AF583371

# EPICS OF HOPE

## An Indian's Reminiscence of Barcelona

**SREE JITH**

**AUTHOR**

EPICS OF HOPE

 This book is a work of fiction. The characters, events and the incidents are either the product of the author's imagination or are used fictitiously. Any resemblance to actual persons, living or dead, events or locales is entirely coincidental

Contact Info: stsnair007@gmail.com

Book Cover Design by: Shakir, Freelancer

Edition: Third 2024

Dedicated to my biggest motivators
Rincy, Vasi, Priya, Vaishu & everyone else, connected with me through the noble bond of friendship.

Thanks to Tania, Yuliia, Arun & Deepa who contributed to this book by guiding me with new life experiences.

To my mom & my piece of heart, Jazarika.

&

To everyone who loves me, hurt me & healed me.

# CONTENTS

# FOREWORD

Epics of Hope is a poignant exploration of the human experience through the lens of pain, love, trust, and hope. Authored by Sreejith, this collection of stories delves deep into the intricacies of emotions, inviting you to embark on a journey into the perspectives of the writer through the several characters portrayed in the story— characters whose lives are marked by memorable moments of joy, sorrow, hope, and despair.

From the cultural gap in how romantic relationships are perceived to the enduring echoes of past traumas that linger in the depths of the subconscious to the portrayal of love through the eyes of ego and lack of trust, each story offers a window into the complexities of the human heart.

The book subtly expresses the fact that somewhere between holding on and letting go, there is always a ray of hope. It serves as a stark reminder that the human heart is capable of growth, healing, and redemption, even in the face of seemingly insurmountable odds.

Hope and time complement each other. Time relies on hope to power a person through difficult times, while hope, in turn, relies on time's healing nature to lessen the impact of lost hope. With heartfelt wishes to Sreejith for writing this collection of moving stories, I invite you to immerse yourself in the world of "Epics of Hope".

**Abhishek Krishnan**
**Author**

# PREFACE

The twists and turns of rollercoaster life consistently whisk away people to places and experiences that are unexpected. My journey from Trivandrum, a quaint town in the south of India, to one of the most vibrant cities in the world, Barcelona, has exposed me to a series of such rollercoasters. The ones that stayed close to my heart have shaped my perspective, inspiring me to pen down this collection of stories set against the backdrop of this city.

*Epics of Hope* comprises four tales that voyage through four seasons, capturing the emotions inherent to the most magnificent magician in the world—time. Each story presents a unique journey—the wintry grip of grief, an unfinished romance of autumn, a cultural shock of summer reflecting the clash of traditions and expectations in a foreign land, and a trance of optimism that buds with spring.

The end of each story reflects ordinary human life and allows the reader to redefine their fantasies or how they want to feel.

You will find references to historical events, mythology from India, movies, songs, and television premiers, which I think would open the doors to a new universe of cultural integration.

While *Epics of Hope* is a work of fiction, it draws upon real-life experiences and observations, inviting readers to navigate the blurred lines between reality and imagination. I wish I could replay and edit the events of life if it had a rewind button. Through the lens of storytelling, I explore themes of love, loss, and the eternal dance between hope and despair. I hope these narratives will resonate with readers, offering solace, inspiration, and perhaps a newfound perspective.

With gratitude to all who have played a part, directly and indirectly, in bringing this book to fruition, I warmly welcome you, dear reader, to my world of words.

# PEANUTS

## A Winter Story

Barcelona froze in the grasp of its winter. From a distance, Mount Carmel gleamed white with narrow valleys and grove of trees, resembling a scoop of vanilla ice cream sprinkled with green and brown sugar crumbs. This snowfall was the first of 2022, perhaps the last as well for the insomnolent city that cuddled the Mediterranean Sea. The cold inside and outside Kateryna's body were more intense than the chill of the snowfall. She wore a beautiful bridal gown, perhaps a relic of her wedding day. After all these years, it wasn't easy to ascertain whether the gown was indeed from that momentous occasion. No one alive could commemorate how beautifully she walked down the aisle holding her uncle's hand on the day of her wedding, when she became Ivan's forever.

Some weddings served only as reminders of sore recollections rather than joyous celebrations, as was the case of Kateryna. Her father was not there to hold her hand and walk down the aisle since she lost him during the great famine of the 20th century, a catastrophe of staggering proportions. It was often compared to the Holocaust in its magnitude and devastation.

Was that a natural or a created famine?

The exact origins of this *famine*[2] remained ambiguous and controversial, with questions lingering about whether it was a natural disaster or a product of human manipulation and neglect.

Kateryna's recollection of this harrowing period was a recurring theme in her conversations. I could remember her repeating this story a million times, wholly or in bits and pieces, despite the dementia that encroached on her in later life.

The first occasion I could remember was, when I had my menarche, then, when I acted as Juliet at my school theatre wearing a beautiful white gown, then again, when I told her about my first boyfriend, when I briefly decided to get married but pulled back, and many more. The commonalty was, all those moments accompanied me with pain and fear.

Whenever I listened to her tale, I felt the emotions woven into the fabric of her words.

Her frozen body now rested in a black coffin with golden handles, adorned with flowers in her favourite colours and scents. Anyone who walked into that Catholic church could never doubt, even in the deepest trenches of their hearts, why so many irises, blue roses, and blue delphiniums surrounded her. The flowers around her deeply signified the blues of her life and the ocean of emotions in her heart. Her melancholic childhood filled with the fear of war, hunger and uncertainty, likely fostered her deep love for blue flowers, which apparently became an integral part of her life. Bittersweet casket sprays decorated the coffin chosen by our family, lovingly arranged around her. Even at ninety-six, she resembled a classic morpho butterfly, her wings as pure as her name, 'Kateryna'—a sight that could undoubtedly make Ivan fall in love with her again if they were to meet beyond the seven skies.

Some bereavements had nothing to offer but unforgettable agony. I wondered if it was ever possible to remember the departure of a beloved soul as a blissful one? One of my

Indian friends, Umesh, once amused me with the tales of saints and sages in the Himalayas who purportedly left their earthly forms ascending to heaven as souls.

Umesh was my best friend once, a partner in crimes. But alas, our paths diverged after a disagreement over survivorship bias when he audaciously compared his work to Ms Rowling's Harry Potter—an absolute masterpiece.

Was that the true catalyst behind why we didn't speak or meet afterwards?

Totally unrealistic to believe so. Indeed, there lurked deeper currents beneath the surface, reasons left unexplored and unexamined.

Judging human nature was like judging a fruit by its skin. Some looked ripe but were sour or bitter inside, while others appeared raw but were perfectly ripe within. The true flavor could only be discovered by peeling and tasting.

Whatever— the story about the saints seemed incredibly farfetched! Too awful!! How can people be so naive and superstitious, especially after receiving a good education? I always argued that education was the key to dispelling such beliefs, but it appeared that this was not always the case, even in the modern world.

Perceptively, another doubt echoed in my brain. Even if the story of sages were true, could those demises ever be remembered as delightful memories by their loved ones? For ordinary humans, it would typically require an immense amount of time to fill those voids created by the detachments.

Nadia?"

I abruptly woke up from the trance, where I found myself entangled in a debate with my convictions, and turned around.

"When you return home, could you also grab the photograph on Mama's bedside table? She would want that with her."

Andrei told me with a whisper after coming close to me, with a trembling that announced his most profound pain. For a

moment, it sounded like a wind blowing through a great musician's flute without creating any soothing music.

"Si *Tato*[4]"

I used to believe that I shared the strongest bond with *Baba*[4]. However, this day began stirring up a blend of emotions within me. Throughout all these years, I had never witnessed Tato's eyes welling up with tears. He had always been resilient, holding himself together with his unwavering and determined personality, playing the role of the breadwinner for our family through every tough decision we had to face, including his divorce.

He was the youngest among the three sons Kateryna and Ivan brought onto this planet, followed by Ruslan and Evgen, yet he was the toughest. Thirty years ago, when he made the boldest decision to relocate the entire family along with his parents to Spain, it marked as one of the most challenging decisions of our lives. We had to bid farewell to our homeland and embark on a new journey in a foreign land, unfamiliar with its language and culture. I was just a few months old when we settled in Barcelona. He often claimed that it was for my best we moved here and that hope persisted within me. However, I sometimes wondered if it was, especially while communicating with Spaniards or people from other nationalities. I still found it difficult to understand people in this part of the world adequately, in spite of spending so many years here. Some friends, including Uma, often criticized me for being too direct. But I disagreed. Instead of sugar-coating the words, it was always best to speak plainly.

While others may prefer spontaneity, I preferred planning, which often gave me an upper hand and a backup plan in case of failure. These traits may have been inherited and passed down through my genetics. Unpretentiously, they had their advantages and disadvantages, but I never regretted them. On the contrary, I observed how people spend half their lives trying to charm others, only to spend the other half dealing with the anxieties caused by those very people.

As I settled into the car and began driving, I couldn't help but wonder why Barcelona remained teeming with tourists, even during those freezing days. They swarmed around the ARC de TRIOMF like bees around a hive, with a substantial buzzing noise that did not annoy me much with my wandering mind and closed window glasses. A strong cold wind was blowing as if the world was awaiting an apocalypse.

Screech!!

I pressed the brake pedals so hard with a squealing noise right before the pedestrian crossing. It jolted me awake from my palace of memories, leaving me to wonder how I could have allowed myself to be so absent-minded while driving. But how did this happen?

Was that muscle memory? Or did I practice being absent-minded unintentionally while driving?

Perhaps it was the latter, but the accusing glares from a few pedestrians made me feel as though I had already run them over.

Shaking off the momentary panic, I noticed several food delivery workers seated on the pavement of Calle de Princesa.

Among them were Pakistanis, Indians, Bangladeshis, and individuals of other nationalities, a familiar sight from past experiences and debates.

I wondered how these individuals from India and Pakistan managed to socialize together despite the hostility and tensions between their countries. I presumed that it should be merely their shared profession that brought them together, surpassing national divides.

"Planta quatre."

The elevator in my parents' apartment always screamed in a loud Catalan lady's voice, which grated my ears every time I walked in.

Thoughts swirled in my mind—

Did I park the car in the right spot?

Were all the doors locked? Ah, but of course, that's automatic.

Overwhelmed with a huge breath, I wondered how the entire drive seemed to pass by in a blur, like it was guided by some unseen force, like an Artificial Intelligence.

"Pfff…"

When I opened the door of that apartment, for the first time I felt, my heart was about to stop, breaking all zones of its cardio. The realization that I would not see my baba anymore, struck me like a sledgehammer—the one who had been there every time I opened that door for the past three decades.

Introspection immersed me in a sense that consumed only my emotions for the past few hours.

The stark shadows of truth enveloped my pupils, sapping the strength from my limbs until they felt incapable of supporting my body. Desperately, I clung to the arms of the blue couch positioned across from the television in the living room. That was her favourite spot, where she sat to watch her beloved television shows. I was able to sense her arms under my trembling palms, with no pulse or flow of blood anywhere in my body. Like the couch itself, I felt myself turning blue with a wave of cold emptiness creeping inside. Sinking to the floor beside the couch, I rested my head upon its arms as if they were her arms, leaning onto them, seeking a solitary solace from her embrace. Tears might not require blood flow, pulses, or senses; they flowed down my cheeks vigorously, wiping down every bit of makeup left on my face from the previous night.

I did not know how long I had sat there. All my ability to drive a car, run, walk, or even breathe seemed lost. I looked at my mobile phone, scrolling through the contacts to find the number of a friend who lived in the neighbourhood. Umesh. The guy who was readily available with fewer plans.

"Uma."

"Si Nadia, qué tal?" he answered in a doubtful voice for a totally unexpected call.

"If you are free, please come to my parents' place? I want you to drive me back to the church."

"Are you all right?"

"No, my grandmother passed away this morning…" I trembled.

"Don't worry! I am on my way!" The unplanned guy spontaneously answered without even a tiny bit of hesitation in his mind.

After a few seconds of silence, the call perished. No further responses were required from either end.

I continued sitting there waiting for Uma without track of time. Time moved slowly like in another planet or some other multi-dimensional time-dilation space.

Breaking the room's silence, birds in the wall clock came out cuckooing a few times, then a few more. I got up slowly, regaining all my strength and accepting the sad truth of life, and walked into her room. Perhaps it was the first time I had entered her room in her absence. I could not remember any other instance when that had happened before. Every memory in that room was connected only to her.

A tidy room greeted me, adorned with nothing more than a bed, a wardrobe, a reading table, and a bedside table. A long white umbrella with blue flowers hung on the yellow gradient wall. The bed remained neatly made, with the pillows perfectly arranged. Beside the bed, a pair of furred slippers laid, awaiting Kateryna's return. On the reading table, a couple of books and a diary sat, untouched for at least five years, yet meticulously dusted. Her reading glasses and a fountain pen also rested right next to the diary.

On the bedside table, there was nothing except a family photograph of Baba with Tato, Mama, and me. I could vividly recall when that photograph was taken. It was my graduation day at the university. Tato had the idea of bringing Baba to the university, perchance the only time she had set foot inside such an institution in her entire life.

Nostalgia, one of the strongest human weaknesses, often traps life in a time loop, pouring out emotions of joy and success, but mostly loss. The concept of perfect life certainly is the most unrealistic oxymoron in the English vocabulary. Debating about that would be like, writing the story of perfectness on the sands of a shore that each passing tide or a more significant wave can wash away. Learning to rejoice in every moment when it's present would be a profound way to cherish and appreciate the beauty of that uncertainty.

"Ding, dong!"

The apartment's doorbell emitted a harsh sound that was intended to startle me with shock, like how it was for the dogs, cats, birds, and other animals during Sant Joan in Barcelona.

Uma patiently waited as I made my way to the front door at a snail's pace.

"Hey," I said.

He hugged me without uttering a word that radiated a warmth of love throughout my body. It carried a blend of maternal, paternal, and fraternal affection, a characteristic deeply ingrained in this young man. I had seen glimpses of it before: the way this fellow sat with the homeless on the streets, the eagerness he expressed to feed them with the bit of money he had, and most importantly, his efforts to instil hope over long conversations, losing track of time in the process.

“I’m sorry,” he murmured in my ears, his hand gently stroking the hair at the back of my head.

“Thank you”

“What are you doing here? You should be at the church.

“Hmm. Uma, I came to pick a photograph we wanted to send with Baba’s coffin,” I trembled.

“I can’t do this alone; thank you for coming!”

“Nah! Anytime cariño.” He nodded his head in the typical Indian way.

We walked into Baba’s room again. This time, without much waiting, I took the photograph and put it in my handbag.

“Can you drive me to the church?” I turned over and asked.

He nodded his head positively and continued with a question, his eyes scanning the room.

"Nadia, look," Uma exclaimed, pointing towards the wall near the wardrobe. "A lot of ants are coming out of there."

I swung open the wardrobe door and peered inside, where I saw, among the clothes, a small polyethene cover partially opened and brimming with peanuts. The ants scurried around, carrying bits and pieces of the snack like a miniature parade, showcasing the might of their tiny army.

With a heavy heart, I retrieved the cover and dropped it into the nearby dustbin. The thought of carrying it to the kitchen felt burdensome—my heart weighed heavier than my body.

"Why was it there?" Uma curiously asked me, his eyebrows furrowed in doubt.

Like many other stories Baba told, this was also an important one in her life. The only story she never forgot to repeat, maybe because it was the most important one.

A story about hunger, pain, fear, tear, loss, deaths, bread, gun fires, butt hits, wheat fields, whippings, forgotten truth, hidden facts, prisoners, missing people, survivors, and many more.

It was a tale that unfolded in a small village in Cherkasy Oblast, in a country that loved sunflowers, even before Kateryna crossed paths with Ivan and well before most of us alive today were born.

The most vivid version of that tale in my memory dates back to the day I started menstruating. As I struggled in pain, Baba told me a story even more agonizing, making my squirming seem as insignificant as a tiny grain in a vast stack of wheat.

She was merely six years old when it unfolded, but the way she narrated every time made me realize the aftershocks and trauma it inflicted on her and the impact it created in people's lives. It was far worse, surpassing the comprehension of anyone who resided in a city like Barcelona in the last century.

The emotions tied to that tale could only be felt with immense pain, never fully grasped, no matter how many times it was retold. Like a Nolan movie, we see them, enjoy every bit, and celebrate the victories, but after coming out of the cinemas, there would always be a series of questions on how, what, or was that even possible? Finally, it was my turn to narrate!

I glanced at Uma; my voice lacked its usual volume and confidence. The burden of heartache drained all my energy, particularly from my vocal cords. Gently, I traced the wall with my fingertips, following the trail of the planet's longest-living insects without disturbing their procession.

"Uma, did I mention to you that my family lived in Ukraine until I was born, and later, my tato decided to move us here?"

Uma nodded his head, acknowledging his awareness.

"Long ago, my Baba shared a story from her life with me; she recounted it to me multiple times. These ants and the peanuts are the residuals of that story."

# I

# The Memoirs of a Tragedy

One day, Baba went to Nadia's room when she was in anguish. Sitting beside her, she gently cradled Nadia's head in her lap, running her fingers through her hair. Those were the days before her dementia set in, when she was still healthy, like a strong river that flowed over all the rocks that tried to block her, so powerful that it could even break a dam if one were ever constructed to impede its course.

"Nadia, don't worry, child. It is just for a few days and then again for a few days, another few days, and again a few more days until you get used to it, and this becomes a part of your life. Don't expect any man to understand this pain; they never will!" Baba said, chuckling softly.

"Hmm." Nadia could not giggle like her, so she just hummed out her response.

"I am going to tell you a story in which my tato Heorhiy, Mama Olesya, my *sestra*[4] Odarka, my brat Maksym, my sestra Orynko. It's a tale of terrifying months and years, teetering between life and death, much like a mouse caught between its food and the trap."

Her narration began in a voice with explicit pain.

"It was the beginning of a blue and bleak winter in my village, Dzenzelivka; the entire village was slowly turning into a graveyard because of poverty and brutality. This was years before the terrors of the Second World War spread. Some said that it was a famine, and some affirmed it as a collectivization policy of the government, yet all I understood was that my tato and uncles toiled hard in the fields to put bread on our table. Still, they could not because all the crops they grew were taken away by someone else.

Baba took a short silence, which made her look stronger so she could narrate the rest of her life story.

One day, a bunch of people called themselves a brigade walked into our house. On their way in, they pushed Tato onto the floor and screamed something I didn't understand.

They called us *kulaks*[3] and nailed a picture forcefully on our wall.

The picture of a man with a big moustache, dressed in Khaki with war medals all over it—in collars, chest, and peak cap. All I knew was that he never looked like a kind man. Before leaving, they went inside the kitchen, hastily gathered various stuff into a small jute sack, and on their way back they kicked Tato in his face.

Mama wept as she spent the entire evening applying medicine from the bushes to Tato's face. One of his eyes had swollen to a fiery red, with a deep blue bruise beneath it, resembling an ocean of pain. I couldn't bear to look at his face for long. After a brief rest, Tato went outside with immense pain inside and outside.

Until Tato returned, we went without anything to eat, leading me to believe there was nothing left in the kitchen. As darkness fell, Tato returned with only a tiny amount of flour, far from enough to ease our hunger.

In the shadow of night, I overheard Mama consoling Tato, mentioning that at least we had a cow, while our neighbour Mykhailo had even less, struggling to provide for his three sons and daughters. Throughout the night, Tato's subdued groans echoed; I was sure he was trying to shield his family from the fear of pain that might weaken their willpower, knowing we needed to fight it out together."

Nadia held Baba's hands gently and moved them to her chest. She was already feeling the trembling and pain of her grandmother. Kateryna continued her narration, it was just the beginning of something worse.

In the days that followed, our home fell into quiet misery. Occasionally, we got a little bread, sometimes cheese or milk, but we needed more to satisfy the hunger of all six of us. My sole source of joy was playing with my friend Yashka, Mykhailo's son, and his dog Hector, a lively white and brown medium-sized canine.

Playing with Hector made us forget about our hunger. He was adored by everyone in the family—Tato, Mama, Odi, Maksy, and Ori. For most of the day, Hector would accompany Yashka to our house.

Mykhailo's poverty was apparent. Back in the day, whenever Yashka and Hector visited, Mama used to offer them something to eat. We always had enough bread and cheese in our home. However, she didn't have that generosity anymore. I didn't ask her why because I understood that we had been struggling and we never had enough food on the table. I had witnessed Tato and Mama going to bed hungry many nights, sacrificing their meals so that we children could eat.

One morning, Mykhailo came rushing to our house, calling my name at the top of his lungs.

"Katia! Katia!! Come quickly. I can't find Hector anywhere." he exclaimed—his voice filled with panic.

"Oh! My god!" I responded, my heart sinking with dread.

"Last night we had meat after a long time. I had my fill, and then I wanted to give some to Hector, but he was nowhere to be found. I asked my tato, and he said Hector was playing outside. But when I looked this morning, he was gone,"

Yashka explained, his disappointment evident on his face.

Yashka and I searched tirelessly for Hector throughout the morning. By the afternoon, I was starving; Yashka, having eaten well the night before, seemed stronger. But both of us couldn't stop our tears, which streamed down our faces uncontrollably. As young children, we felt helpless and lost. Unsure of what more we could do to find our beloved dog, we decided to seek help from the adults.

"Someone told me that a wolf came into our village last night. Hector may have run away, fearing the animal. Don't worry! He will come back soon."

While saying that, the eyes of Yashka's Mama were filled with tears.

That night, sleep eluded me for many reasons. Not only was I kept awake by the hunger from the tiny bit of bread I had for dinner, but also by the nagging questions spinning inside my head.

Where could Hector have gone?

Would he come back like Yashka's Mama said?

And if he didn't, what could I possibly do to make Yashka happy?

That was not required; Yashka and family, who had a good supper with meat again that night, never woke up from their sleep.

Hector never came back.

Yashka was buried directly in the ground along with his tato and mama without a coffin. I cried, standing there until dark. I cried inconsolably, feeling the weight of the loss of my dear friend and his family. The tears kept flowing even after Mama took me home.

The same night, I heard Mama crying and whispering to Tato in the coldest depth of darkness.

"Heorhiy, please never do what Mykhailo had to do with his family. I don't want…. Our children…"

Olesya could not complete her words. Our sobbing continued until the moon stopped illuminating the world that was no longer ours.

Days passed by; Hunger and fear of death felt like a blessing that made me forget Yashka and Hector.

I searched the fields and forests for any scraps of food I could find, gathering acorns, dried berries, and nuts. I hid them in secret places at home because I was scared of the *requisition brigades*[6], who could have marched in at any time and confiscated them. I ate them only when I was famished, and most of the time, I shared them with my sisters and brothers, too, still holding my reserves.

Months passed, and our situation grew from bad to worse. Tato could only bring home a scant amount of flour for bread, leaving Mama and Ory, the eldest sister, no choice but to join him in the fields. Each day, they were allowed to carry a tiny sheaf of wheat with a maximum of a few stems, typically five or six, barely enough for a single piece of bread.

One fateful day, out of hunger, Ory stole an extra sheaf and hid it under her clothes, which unfortunately fell into the eyes of a brigade. While leaving work, the brigade, along with the police, stopped and inspected her, only to find the hidden sheaf under her clothes and apprehended. Odi and I, watching from afar, rushed to her aid, our hearts pounding with fear and desperation.

All we could see when we approached was the grim sight of Ory bound to a pole, her bare back exposed to the relentless blows of a man with eyes like burning coals, wielding vicious whiplashes, beating out every bit of flesh that remained in her soft white skin, turning them to blue and red without an inch to spare.

Ory's screams echoed through the air, along with her desperate pleading to cease from the top of her pain. She only had enough flesh to hold her bones together and nothing more. Even that had been stripped out of her bones. Perhaps the blood wanted to ooze out of her wounds like a jet spray, but she didn't have enough of that either.

Mama threw herself at the feet of the brigades and pleaded at those deaf ears to stop the lashes while her tears slowly washed away all the dirt in the shoes of those monsters. Instead of showing any mercy, the brigade kicked Mama with his strong winter boots to the ground, where she shrunk like a foetus inside a womb who lost hope to come out to a horrifying world filled with brutality and injustice.

All Odi and I could do was stand there, frozen in horror, our voices lost in the screams of Ory's agony. We clung to each other, our hearts breaking with every blow that rained down upon our sister.

At last, the assault stopped, leaving behind a silence after the world got engulfed in an apocalypse caused by a massive hail storm that crushed every life on its way. The brigade threatened to move us to the *gulags*[5] if it repeated.

They untied Ory, unquestionably not because of kindness. Apparently, they would have already met their quota of suffering and pillaging kids from the countryside for the day.

We carried Ory home, her body racked with pain and her spirit broken, unsure how to hold her. Every step was agony, her wounds burning with an immense fire that seemed to consume her from within. The whole way, the remaining day and the entire night, she wept bitterly for her cruel fate, for being unlucky—with pain, hunger, and fear.

Wounds from the flogging on her back swelled and throbbed with pain. It was asking, "Why was I even born in this world?" They looked like the chrysalis of a butterfly from where the wings were about to break out, crushing its shell to fly away as an angel to emerge into this world with newfound freedom.

I sat beside her the entire night and wished if it happened if she could fly high into the clouds and higher to another world where she could eat, sleep, and play happily, and also, she could come back for us and carry us one by one to that world beyond the skies, mountains, and oceans.

And somewhere between those thoughts, I fell asleep.

The following day, I woke up hearing the cries of Mama, Odi, and Maksy. Tato was standing next to them with eyes brimming with unshed tears.

I touched Ory. She was freezing, in fact, colder than the ice that fell during the hail storm that should have caused the apocalypse last evening.

Ory had emerged with greater strength out of her chrysalis, when her wings grew big enough to shadow the moon. She broke free from the earthly shackles, and ascended to the heavens above.

Do we all get to go there as well?

Tears welled up in my eyes, cascading down my cheeks like the swollen waters of the Dnipro River in flood.

Baba became motionless for a few seconds; her hands were trembling. A few tears escaped her eyes, landing softly on Nadia's cheeks. Nadia gently rose from Baba's lap, embracing her tightly with a heavy heart.

Sitting beside Baba, she draped her arms over her shoulders and leaned onto it.

Baba continued.

"After Ory was gone, one of Tato's relatives invited us to live with them in their village, which was already involved in some government policy. We were made to work like donkeys but got just enough bread to keep us alive. Somewhere in those disastrous days, Tato also fell ill and departed from this world, leaving us to suffer alone.

Every day, we kept hearing terrifying stories about the famine, which sent shivers down our spine. Some people ate tree bark; some ate earthworms, frogs, roots, leather boots, pigeons, mushrooms, acorns, and anything else they could find to quell their hunger; tragically, some even took their own lives.

Some people scavenged unconsumed grains from horse manure in a desperate bid to survive. All the good people had to die first because they could neither eat corpses, hide or hoard food, nor they could harm others. Some parents made the agonizing decision to let their weak children pass away to let others live.

To survive, some people became cannibals; some didn't, and they died sooner than their children.

Lucky were those who could hide at least a chicken in their house because the requisition brigades took away everything, sometimes even young girls.

Nobody knew how many people died. Three and a half million?

Seven million?? Twelve million???

For what? Just because they owned the lands they cultivated?"

Baba's tone changed from distress to anger.

"Some people still believe that it was not a man-made famine. Like a great man once said – it is easy to fool people, but it is difficult to convince them that they are fooled."

# II
# The Last Parade

As I concluded Kateryna—my Baba's story, a solemn hush descended upon the room, heavy with the weight of her emotions conveyed through my words. Uma and I looked at each other, our eyes reflecting the emotions of those who endured in Dzenzelivka. It felt as if we travelled back in time to that village, reliving the anguish and resilience that permeated every aspect of Kateryna's story, which resonated deeply through my narration.

"Let's go!" Uma told enveloping me in a comforting embrace.

Without answering, I took the photograph encased in a silver frame from Baba's table. This cherished relic of past memories had rested in that table for countless years. Baba's firm gaze captured in that image, seemed to pierce through me with the intensity of a thousand suns. Those eyes held not only immense strength and determination but also a warmth of kindness, empathy, love, and peace.

We closed the door of that apartment on the fourth floor and walked towards the car. During that walk, I handed over the keys to Uma involuntarily like a silent choreography honed over years of friendship, which was one of the rituals embedded in our routine. We had countless topics to discuss, argue, or debate, such as JK Rowling, the mystique of Himalayan sages, or the plight of Barcelona's Street beggars. However, inside the car, a serenity covered us like a hidden cloud punctuated only by the soft humming of the engine and the wind from the air conditioner.

The doors opened and closed twice at the church.

Approaching the casket, I carefully placed the photograph between Baba's chest and her clasped palms. A solitary tear from my eyes fell on her palms like a gentle plea to awaken her from her final sleep. Baba was also ready to break her chrysalis, pull her wings out, and emerge into this world to repeat the brutal, barbaric fragment of her life that tells the story of humankind, which was left to suffer, experiment, die, kill, steal, forced to cannibalism, prostitution, poverty, and humiliation.

A few pages of everyone's life might sound like fiction and would be unbelievable for those who never travelled on that trail. Perceptions of incidents are merely illusions that stand between the lines of truth and lie. Sometimes, it looks presumably, the interpretations are glorified. However, experiencing them diminishes pride and doubts over time and brings back the reality of true realization.

The bearers respectfully stepped back from the bier following the interment. The mourners, having paid their last respects, gradually moved away.

My thoughts started seeking a sense of closure as the first fist of sand fell on the coffin. Baba's casket was shut along with harrowing truths, the agony of loss, and the grief of millions.

The beautiful black box adorned with the blue casket spray, symbolizing both oceans and sky, now became a vessel holding not just Baba, but the weight of countless stories and sorrows. A headstone was erected that stood tall, bearing the elegant inscription—

'Kateryna Kozak, beloved wife of Ivanov Kozak,' marking the span of her legacy for all eternity.

Umesh hugged me comfortingly and walked away slowly without uttering a word.

Tato and I became the last people standing before her, harking back to all the memories she bestowed upon this planet. The sky too darkened prematurely, supposedly paying its silent homage.

Tato drove the car back home. Upon reaching, once more I stepped into Baba's room in her absence. When dementia and old age bothered her mind, resurfacing the horrors of her past, Baba found solace in the simple act of hiding nuts and dried fruits throughout her room, much like the six-year-old girl from Dzenzelivka, who sought comfort amidst adversity.

I sat on her bed once again with tears clouding my eyes and my mind racing through the thoughts of my reminiscences with her. The parade of ants still continued to emerge from the crack in the wall, carrying the bits and pieces of her soul to a realm of abundance.

# SHE IS A POEM

## An Autumn Story

The morning sun cast its golden rays upon Mount Tibidabo, transforming its snowy peaks into glistening white pearls that shimmered like a radiant full moon. It awakened a renewed sense of vibrancy dissipating every bit of negativity around this musical Ciudad. People strolled through the narrow streets with broad smiles lit up on their faces.

Some exchanged warm greetings and well wishes to those with whom they intertwined their eyes with an unintended intention to melt away their sorrows, boost their expectations, or meet their ends. Some carried the melody of their favourite tunes in their ears through headphones; in contrast, others paused to listen to the melodies of street musicians, whose soulful performances echoed through the metro pathways and under the canopy of winter trees.

For Manel, it was a momentous day filled with anticipation and anxiety. His heart pounded with a mix of hope and fear as he hurried along, with the sound of his footsteps resonating loudly in his ears.

"Come on, man! You need to walk faster, or even run— you might never get another chance," he muttered, urging his legs to move quicker. With unwavering determination, he forged ahead through the crowd, his destination firmly etched in his mind.

The director and the producer waited for him in the Star Bucks, which was right opposite to the illustrious Casa Batlló—a masterpiece crafted by the renowned architect *Antoni Gaudi*[1]. Its captivating beauty was a testimony to Gaudi's genius. Manel had often found himself drawn to the Casa Batlló, each encounter leaving him yearning for more time to bask in its splendour. Yet, on this occasion, he hurried past, oblivious to its enchanting allure, without sparing a single gaze.

A vast crowd, predominantly Chinese tourists, swarmed before the Casa Batlló, obstructing Manel's path. It seemed this mass had appeared from a distant corner of globe solely to delay his progress on that particular morning.

"WTF!" he muttered, his frustration mounting as he manoeuvred his way through the crowd and hurried past.

"Oh, God, it's already 10:00 o'clock. I promised the director I'd be here by now. If they were Spanish, I could get away with being a few minutes late. After all, I'm a Catalan living in Catalunya, the bustling heart of Barcelona. The producer, Hannah Whitbread, is English."

Manel soliloquized while he pushed open the massive door of Star Bucks and scanned the coffee shop with his grey eyes.

Danny Roberts enthusiastically waved from a corner table seemingly they were expecting him for a while. Manel navigated through the bustling café, struggling to make his way towards their table. "Good morning, ma'am... morning, Dan," Manel greeted them.

"Bon dia! Amigo. You can call me Hannah," Hannah replied in her typical British accent, rising from her seat to greet Manel with the customary Spanish kisses.

When Danny mentioned Hannah before, Manel hadn't expected her to be so young and pretty. She wore a dark red off-shoulder top showing off her short hair, reminding him of Uma Thurman from *Pulp Fiction*[2]—a unique style indeed. He also noticed her long black winter coat draped over the next chair. She was also tall like a Dutch girl.

"Hah! Unique," Manel mused to himself.

Dan got up from his brown wooden chair and hugged Manel warmly.

"Hey buddy," Dan said.

Manel had known Dan for some years. He had previously worked with him as an assistant director on some movies. Dan was a good guide and a mentor, a typical Hollywood masterpiece.

With his physique, he should be playing Rambo or Rocky and delivering the dialogue—*Hey! It ain't about how hard you get hit.* But I have yet to hear his intend to act. He had always been the guy behind the clapboard.

He owed Manel one for the climax of his last movie, which he was struggling to finish, and now he was here with a new producer to hear the story of what might be my first movie as a director.

"Sorry! To make you guys wait."

"No, not at all! Do you want to grab a coffee or something before you start?" Hannah responded to Manel's reply with a grin.

Manel nodded his head with high eyebrows and walked towards the Café counter.

"A Café Latte with whipped cream and vanilla, please."

The café started becoming less packed faster than usual, a welcome change that day. Mornings were typically bustling here due to the café's prime location. Manel couldn't help but saw it as a positive omen since he entered that place.

As he returned to his seat, Manel pondered how he would present himself. A shave, a trim, and a neatly pressed shirt would have been ideal, but the late-night indulgence in a few bourbons and the malfunctioning water heater had ruined his morning routine.

"Pfff…" he sighed, shaking his head at the thought.

Taking a long breath, Manel retrieved his coffee from the table with a subdued "Thank you." Despite his less-than-ideal start to the day, he walked back to the table with newfound confidence. After all, it wasn't a job interview with Dan and Hannah but rather a creative discussion.

Chances were challenging to come by, and when you find the right one, you should be extra cautious to ensure everything runs smoothly. Manel had meticulously prepared to tell the story. Over the past few days, he had numerous discussions about it with his flatmate and friend Vasilis, alias Vasi. A unique blend of Greek, German, and Iranian heritage made him a genuinely global guy, who was concerned about a lot of bad stuff happening in this world. The thread of the story came from him, perhaps more than just a mere thread.

"Shall we start?" Once again, the heavy Brit accent knocked at Manel's eardrums with a smile.

"Yeah, sure!"

"Do you have a name for it already?" Dan asked.

"Not yet. But I have a few in mind. Can we put those on the table once the discussion is over?" Manel glanced at their faces, gauging their expressions.

"That sounds good, "said Hannah.

Manel continued.

"Before getting into the story, I would like to set a few expectations.

Currently, I have no names for actors in the lead roles. Somehow, this is tied to a true story, and I am still searching for suitable alternatives to their original names. It feels harsh for me since the original ones fit well, but others not much. The narrative will primarily unfold from the perspective of the male lead character, with the female lead referred to as *She* for the time being."

Manel paused for a moment with a faint hope.

"We must catch a flight back to LA this evening, so let's move on. Names and names can be discussed later. Isn't that fine, Hannah?" Dan responded with a sarcastic smile and a wink

"Secondly, the current progression of the narrative and its climax might come across more as an incomplete romantic drama or a philosophical satire. Though it starts as a romantic story, it dives into the intricacies of a relationship from the perspectives of one of the characters. However, for the other lead character, it transforms into a philosophical monologue with the former and latter running in parallel, complimenting each other for the viewers."

Manel started to narrate the story with a cinematic flair.

"The opening scene unfolds outside the Encants metro station in Barcelona's Purple Lane. The camera is set to capture the exit steps leading to Encants."

"Wait! Wait!! Wait!!" Hannah interrupted instantly, which seemed unorthodox for an English woman.

"Does it take place in Barcelona?" A producer's concern for the budget surfaced immediately, even before the narration began.

"Can't we shoot this in the US or maybe the UK? There were beautiful romantic movies from there, like… *Love actually*[3]." She said the name of the movie after a short pause.

"No, Hannah! The story has many emotions and events connected with Barcelona. I can complete the story, and then let's decide if it is feasible to shoot it in LA, London, or elsewhere." He sounded a little upset.

Hannah smiled, tapped on his shoulder, exhibiting her hierarchy, and continued.

"Oh! That's perfectly fine with me. I am so excited to hear the story."

Manel smiled as he flipped through the pages of his script, hoping to explain without further disruptions. However, the script didn't look fresh, at least not from the outside; it was a bunch of dirty white papers, turned and twisted a million times.

"As I mentioned, the story begins at Encants metro station in the purple lane of Barcelona."

# I

# The Enchantress

A six-foot-tall brown guy in his late thirties, hailing from a conservative southern state of India, still striving to adapt and thrive in the open-minded, beautiful city of Barcelona. That's me, in short! Barcelona welcomes everyone, regardless of their colour, nationality, or background. It embraced me with open arms as well. This is my story in this remarkable city of music and wine, filled with ups, downs, and emotional turmoil in the past few days.

It was a drizzly, windy Sunday morning, early enough. I ascended the steps of Encants metro station, one by one, with hefty feet and sullen face, incapable of summoning a smile. Raindrops mingled with my tears, tracing paths down my bearded cheeks as I made my way up the stairs.

*What have I done? Why have I done it?*[4]

The insanely beautiful lyrics by Simon and Garfunkel were banging my eardrums despite no one playing them or me wearing headphones.

In this world of right handers, usually, people cut the nails on their left hand first because it's easy. In contrast, the people who like challenges always cut their right fingernails first. I was always the latter. The sullen face did not suit me; having an expressive face it never masked my genuine emotions with a veil of ambiguity.

For the first time, I noticed that the winter trees had shed, and only the souls of the trees were seen. They were lush green in good old times, like me. Still, I let slip the reality that they had begun shedding their foliage to souls a few weeks ago. This year it occurred without considering the calendar's insistence on changing seasons, still clung to the essence of autumn.

I remember reading somewhere that—*There were decades that happened in months, and then there were months where decades happened.* I met her at the beginning of such a decade near a restaurant in Passeig de Gracia.

I was drinking my favourite Paulaner cervesa and eating the dishes proposed by my foody friend Mo, with a couple of other girls, Mia and Rinku. Mo never disappointed us with the food she suggested—those were the best you could get.

Being a single man, I had all the liberty in this world to look around and find the best girl in town. But it has yet to happen since I often got stuck between these girls" small talk and gossip. The only man in friends of four – it ought to be like that.

"Oh! Look at that man," Mo whispered.

A group of four young women sat across our table in multiple colours. "I liked the one in white – hot! She is really hot," Mo repeated.

I glanced at the table; it was not the one in white that stroked me – the girl who sat next to her—an angel with amazing eyes who flaunted her hair.

It's an arduous task to explain her beauty.

The sharp nose made a flawless bridge between her eyes and mouth, and a couple of rose petals covered the mouth, which we often call lips.

Broad forehead, not sure how many kisses it can accommodate – a million, a trillion, a zillion. A lifetime is not enough for it.

Beauty is said to be in the eye of the beholder. Would there be any beholder out there who can't find this enchantress? If yes, I will call him blind.

I could feel that all the glands in my body started emitting hormones and pheromones that passed through every nerve and vein. My soul took a toll, and astral projected it from my body to fly near her. It was at that moment that her gaze stuck on me. Hours turned into minutes, and minutes into seconds. I wanted to stare at her for hours, love fully.

"No man, no. Don't push her away," I said to myself.

Nature's call—I hit the washroom. When I opened the door, like the sound of destiny, there she was, exploring herself in the mirror. It's no wonder if the mirror also felt embarrassed because of her eternal beauty. My testosterone pumped up.

"Excuse me," I said

"Oh! Sorry!!" She turned around and rushed out.

Come on, man, I wanted to start a conversation with her. Maybe she thought that I wanted to use the sink.

"Mia, I am falling for her – I almost started, and she left. All I heard was a sorry!"

"Hey! – *Budmo*[5]", she saluted in Ukrainian with her cava glass and said – "Somebody has found someone." Mia grinned like the Cheshire cat from the wonderland of Alice.

"They are leaving, leaving…" Rinku told in a husky whispering voice encouraging me to take further steps.

Oh! God. I turned around. Through the doors glass pane, my eyes once again intertwined with hers. She was looking at me. I closed my eyes, took a long gasp and looked outside once again.. They were not seen in front of that foggy glass door anymore—no pink, white, black, or blue robed girls.

# II

# The Courage

I was not one to quickly get emotional, but when it was about things close to my heart, it always hit me right in the senses. Sometimes, I could be a bit of a drama queen (an equivalent term for men in this patriarchal slang language world was yet to be invented), I guess. Nonetheless, there's a side of me that continually strives to speak, analyse, and respond appropriately. To do that, I had to come down from cloud nine and plant my feet firmly on the surface of this blue planet. Pen and paper were my trusty companions when it came to expressing myself accurately. But even they seemed to fail me today.

Among my friends, I was known for my knack for directions. Once I've been to a place alone, I usually never needed the help of *Larry Scott or Sergey Brin*[6]. The day was different. Standing under the Encants metro signboard, I looked around, still trying to figure out which way to go. I couldn't remember the apartment number, and I wasn't sure if she would even open the door for me. My brain was failing me; the signals weren't connecting correctly within the billion nerves inside my head.

My jacket was soaked, my hands felt as cold as a corpse, my vision was blurred, and my ears were burning hot. I could feel myself freezing up, and my mouth was parched, drying down, down, down. With uncertainty gnawing at me, I began walking down a path I assumed was correct. Simon and Garfunkel's voices still echoed in my ears.

***

I didn't see the road, the people, or the lovely dogs passing by; my mind was too busy being swept back to memories of the restaurant. "Dude, perhaps you won't get another chance," Mia said.

I didn't wait for her to complete like I had decided before hours. I didn't even wait to wear my winter jacket in the freezing weather.

I opened the restaurant door and looked around. There she is, walking with her friends 50 meters away. I ran, walked, and ran to catch up with them without minding my breath.

"Excuse me." That was the second one to her that evening.

Everyone turned around at the same time. I didn't know if any bystanders turned around, too, which I was least worried about.

"Yes"

A strong response from the group that came as a chorus startled me.

With all the courage left in me, I pointed at her and said, "I would like to talk to her for a moment."

"Aww!! "

That was an exciting response from the rest of the group

I moved closer to her,

"Hey, I was looking at you in the restaurant."

"Yeah! I saw that." Her response was spontaneous.

"You are gorgeous; I think I want to see you again."

She nodded her head. I could never decode the meaning of that nod, but I wanted to believe that as a Yes.

“I can give you my number—just want to be a gentleman. If you are fine to meet again, you may text me back.”

She gave me her mobile, and I saved my number for her in that small gadget intended to create and destroy relationships.

I said my name and she said hers.

“Are you from the US? Your accent sounds so.”

“No”

“Then where are you from?”

“Guess?” She started playing with me momentarily and then said, “Ukraine.”

That was when I met my Ukrainian girl in a dark alleyway in Barcelona

It was a country at war with Russia. Did I even realize the emotions she would be going through? Would I ever understand that? I didn’t know at that point.

“Bye. I would expect your text.”

“See you soon.”

With the hope that was evoked by her see you soon, I walked back like Harvey Specter—The charming, confident winner from Suits, a television series by Netflix that always boosted my morale.

"Oh! Look who is coming?" Mo exclaimed and continued, "Come on man, tell me – did you get her number?"

"No"

"WTF?" Mo responded again

"I gave her my number and asked her to ping me if she is interested in going out with me," I said

"Wow! See now who the gentleman is!" Mia screamed, got up from her chair, and hugged me.

"She is a Ukrainian"

"Oh! That's icing on the cake," Rinku threw herself up from the chair and joined the group hug.

Before we ended the conversation, the Ukrainian girl responded with her contact card, and all my friends took turns hugging me.

# III

# The First Date

As I walked, it dawned on me that I had been heading in the wrong direction all along. Passing by the Coaliment shop, where I had once bought her favourite Kombucha, I couldn't help but feel the sting of my failed geographical skills. Though the tears welled up in my eyes had somewhat dried, my heart still ached with sorrow.

Turning around, I retraced my steps, each yard feeling like an eternity in the freezing weather. Suddenly, a loud honking startled me—I had absentmindedly stepped into the road, oblivious to the still-red signal. Offering a quick apology to the driver, I hurried past as if nothing had happened.

Lost in memories, I tried to recall if it was indeed the same door I had entered countless times before, both in daylight and darkness. It felt like destiny was beckoning me; the front glass door of her apartment stood wide open apparently someone had been expecting me for hours. With trembling hands and a heavy heart, I entered the building and headed towards the elevator. Despite the automatic closure of the doors, I couldn't muster the courage to press the button for the second floor. Reminiscences flooded back, reminding me of another monumental door I had opened for her at El Nacional restaurant just a month ago.

***

"Could you please find a seat for me and this beautiful lady?" I asked the waitress

"Sure – a moment, please," She responded.

We found ourselves seated at a charming table positioned at the very heart of the restaurant as though a spotlight had been cast upon us. The place was less of a restaurant and more of a grand palace, with a sprawling interior divided into distinct culinary sections. Upon arrival, guests were escorted to their designated cuisine areas based on reservations and availability.

Amidst all stood a magnificent flower display; it was so exquisitely arranged that neither she nor I dared to disturb them, thinking whether they were real or crafted from plastic.

With my modest understanding of European cuisine, I was determined not to risk spoiling the evening. Hence, following her lead, I opted for a salad speciality as a safe choice. It was accompanied by a few glasses of wine, hoping to savour both the flavours of the food and her company. There was no scarcity of topics for the dinner of our first official date.

Wind energy, global warming, arts, literature, movies, and even the Ukraine-Russia war. Our evening gave me the impression of having a meet-up with a friend who shared the same vibe and was quite unlikely as a date. I felt as that I was conversing with an influential entrepreneur or a professor of political science. Despite the unconventional topics on a first date, one thing remained constant: I couldn't tear my eyes away from her beauty. Her intelligence and charisma created a mirage effect on me, humbling my ego and leaving me feeling captivated. As we talked, I felt myself melting like wax in the warmth of her presence, emitting an unknown scent while being enveloped one another by their intoxicating pheromones.

"Shall we head out? I have work tomorrow," she asked with a tone that had a level of politeness rarely encountered.

"Yes, of course." We paid the check and walked out.

Once again, I opened the big door for her.

"Can you hold this for me?" I stretched out my empty fist as soon as we exited out of the restaurant to her "Yes", she replied.

She opened her palms to hold the oxygen inside my fist. The trick worked—the next moment, I grasped her hand. Our fingers intertwined effortlessly, whispering silent promises of a more profound connection waiting to blossom between us, to get closer to developing the most beautiful relationship this universe could offer. Without the famous *mushrooms from Kodai*[7] of India, the colours painted the world in hues more vivid and surreal than ever before in front of my eyes. A rainbow with more than seven colours followed me in the alley towards the road from El Nacional restaurant.

It was the first day of my life when I lost my geographical skills. We kept holding our hands with those intertwined fingers which tried to make love with each other. As we strolled down the pathway at the centre of Passeig de Gracia, passing by Casa Batlló, navigating through traffic signals, and weaving between trees and streetlights, time seemed to have lost its significance. My mind, reluctant to let go of the moment, stretched every second, like it was unwilling to bring our enchanting walk to an end.

The trees were dancing in the breeze from the Mediterranean Sea, and the streetlights were smiling at us.

"Hey, we are heading in the wrong direction. We need to walk the opposite way," she said

I turned around and gazed at her eyes for a moment.

My lips drew towards her, and the sensation of a million big bangs passed through my head. As our lips met, time seemed to stand still, and we shared a kiss that transcended the bounds of time and space. It felt as if we were breathing each other's essence, our connection deepening with each passing moment. Neither of us wanted that wonderful moment to come to an end.

We woke from the trance and slowly walked towards the metro station, kissing at every new step—the elevator, escalator, street corner, church steps, pavements, middle of the road daring the speeding vehicles, dancing salsa, spinning, tango, under the yellow street lamps, stairs up, stairs down and anywhere that could stir up a memory.

Three mins for the following L2 metro to Encants and La Pau, where we lived.

"Shall we take the next train?" I didn't wait for her answer; we locked our lips once again.

Three, five, eight – minutes passed along with the trains one by one.

Which one did we take? Fourth or the fifth?

How long did we stand like that?

Minutes later, we found ourselves nestled in the comfort of our beds, thinking about the fascinating night we had just shared. Little did we know, this was just the beginning of many more encounters to come—each one more beautiful than the last.

Our days were filled with meaningful meetings, and our nights were nothing short of magical. From passionate hugs of lust to shared moments over coffee and cooking adventures together, our bond grew stronger with each passing day. Despite our differences, we steered through challenges together, facing them head-on with a blend of passion and compassion. While I found myself entangled in the distractions of modern technology, she countered them with her unwavering presence and understanding. Day by day, I dived deeper into her world, slowly unravelling the layers of her complexity.

In the joy of these discoveries, I started failing to cope with my own emotions, struggling to reconcile my unrealistic expectations and manipulative tendencies.

# IV

# The Comet

I entered the elevator and pressed the button for the second floor of her apartment—a heavy silence filled the elevator along with me. The slow ascent seemed to stretch out indefinitely until I reached her floor with a soft chime. Though I had been alone in an elevator a million times before, this was remarkably different. A cloud of anticipation and uncertainty around me created a shadow over my usually calm demeanour.

I stepped out onto the second floor with a sense of unease that I couldn't quite shake.

Out of the many chapters we had in our life, we tend to skip the odd ones even though they demand our attention, compelling us to engage with every twist and turn of the plot, whether we're ready or not; that's how life works. Skipping might look relatively easy for unemotional people, like plucking a flower. But sometimes, the thorns would bruise your arms, lasting forever. We must read every line and meet every character, even if we dislike. Some chapters would bring tears that lasted only a week, while others would haunt us indefinitely. No matter how hard we tried to avoid them, the forces of destiny would inevitably draw us back to revisit those painful passages from time to time.

Exiting the elevator, I found myself facing door number three, a place I had never visited uninvited before. The realization struck me with a pang of devastation, and I couldn't help but wonder if her attraction towards me had been irreparably damaged.

"Ding dong"–once, twice, thrice.

The third time, the angel appeared in front of me in her shaggy pyjamas—Jophiel—the angel of beauty with her wings of charms chopped off already. The Nile of sadness was flowing through the bank of her eyes. This was not the first time I had made her cry. My throat was dry as a desert. Words were not flowing out of my mouth, even though they had never stopped in the past.

We get to see stars every day. Some can shine brightly even in a cloudy sky. Still, we cannot match it with a comet. Comets seldom come. We may see them once in a lifetime or never.

She was one such comet.

She was a brilliant character of emotions, ambitious, and wilfully mighty, like the last deceased majesty of Great Britain. She knew what she wanted and what she didn't.

My heart was immersed in the depth of her eyes once again with the memories of neediness, enthusiasm, and fear of losing her.

***

*Relationships are always worsened by texting.*

Her response to my unhealthy debate through the *devil's gadget*[1] was very mature.

"Let's meet this evening as planned, and we will speak," she said

I indulged in a habit of constantly texting her. That's what all the stars I met before wanted me to do or taught me to do.

- Keep connected.
- Check out now and then.
- Constantly share the pictures.

- Ensure that we are exclusive to each other
- Even track or hack each other's location and contact lists

Is this what a relationship is all about?

It dawned on me, although belatedly, that in the current world, maintaining constant connection was not often a prerequisite for sustaining interest. Here, constant connection would refer to every hour of the day. This had re-written my prejudice that existed without investigating the actuality behind it.

Waiting in front of the mall, I couldn't help but feel a sense of apprehension from the earlier conversation we had. Yet, as soon as she emerged from the metro station, her response was instantaneous and warm.

"Hey, there you are?"

Our embrace felt familiar, as if no time had passed. We settled into our usual spot in front of the Star Bucks in Glories mall, the bustling sounds of shoppers and the aroma of fresh coffee surrounding us, creating a comforting backdrop to our reunion. We kissed and talked like nothing had happened. She delicately sipped her favourite tea, and I enjoyed my café latte with whipped cream and vanilla. The warmth of our beverages mirrored the comfort of our companionship. Yet, again, a nagging sense of neediness crept into my thoughts that was ready to criticize her for not spending time with me, followed by my self-invitation to her apartment.

Her response was silence.

"Do you want to eat? I'd like to introduce you to my favourite restaurant," she asked, staring into my eyes with great affection.

"Why not?" I replied.

"Are you sad?" she asked again. A question she asked many times before and after to check how I felt.

Why didn't I ever do that?

The restaurant, its name now a fleeting memory, provided the perfect backdrop for a beautiful meal shared in her delightful company. As we dived into more conversations that spanned a myriad of topics, her presence enveloped me in a comforting cocoon, momentarily dispelling any feelings of neediness that had lingered within me.

In the warmth of those close moments, we found ourselves departing for the renowned light show in Barcelona. It was there that I was introduced to the concept of a more caring comet, a celestial reminder of the enduring power of compassion and empathy in a world often troubled with chaos and uncertainty.

Standing in the long queue, shivering in the cold and bombarded by harsh flashes of light, my eyes began to redden, a sign of my unidentified allergic condition. Yet, in between that discomfort, a philosophical realization washed over me: the moment I started witnessing a mother in her.

Reflecting on my familial history, I recalled the distant and detached relationship I shared with my parents. From a young age, I was pushed into the role of financial responsibility, assuming the mantle of the family's provider at just 16. My mom and dad were quite cold in their expression of love. I can't remember a single instance from my past when my mom or dad kissed me or said something significant, considering me. Perhaps, they would have done that before I grew up to actually understand the necessity of such emotions.

Even after so many years, I must make the call if I had to speak to my mom. Let it be a week, month, or a year. She never had anything to talk to me except for the money for expenditure or if I ate. That latter may be the only expression of love I ever felt from her, regardless of the passage of time. It's a bitter truth I've learned to push aside, though its sting remains a persistent ache in my heart.

But amongst this emotional void entered the *krasyva*[8]—my gorgeous beacon of light. Her simple gestures, like covering my eyes with a woollen scarf or ensuring I wore a hoodie to shield myself from the harsh light, filled me with a sense of divine solace. It's a feeling that defies expression; only tears can adequately convey the depth of emotion I experienced in those moments.

Her caring nature extended beyond mere gestures, evident in every action she took. Whether caringly responding to my twisted knee while navigating the rugged terrain of Montserrat or proudly sharing a photograph of us with her friends, each interaction was instilled with a sense of genuine care and affection.

It was a contrast to the emotional void I had known for so long, and it filled me with a longing I had scarcely dared to acknowledge until then.

Isn't that what I longed for aeons?

"Oh! It's too late! Do you want a tea with me at my place?" she asked.

"Tea? I want to be with you as long as I can." My heart whispered.

The first selfie with her happened on our way to her apartment, with the *Great Dick of Barcelona*[9] in the background.

A special moment she offered me for life.

That day, when I walked back to meet my friends, once again, I felt like I was flying above the mightiest cloud over Barcelona.

# V

# The Disaster

Staring at her eyes, I struggled for words. I did not have enough tears as they flowed down with the raindrops during the longest walk of my life—from Encants station to her doorstep.

Imagine all the people we have met in our lives. There were so many. They came like waves, tickling our feet, and went out with the tide. A few waves returned during the high tides of life, but a few never.

My struggling for words felt like there would not be a high tide ever after. Where was my confidence and charisma?

I had a letter that I wanted to leave at her doorstep and a pair of new slippers I bought for her.

"I can't have this"

She did not accept the slippers but took the letter, placing it over the heater in the lobby of her house entrance.

Pain seeped in as the words started carrying tears from both of us on their way. I spoke with a dried-down throat for long.

"My attraction is lost, and I can't return to it. Your emotionality is too much for me." She told.

I wondered, if so, why was she crying?

"Leaving all my self-esteem aside, I ask you for one last chance. Why don't we give it a shot again?"

There was no answer. Silence pierced through my eardrums once again. The entire universe went dark for us. I turned around and strolled towards the lift. When I looked back, she had already shut the door.

Was that the end? What did I do to not deserve another chance??

I wonder if she had ever read that letter. Did she tear it off?

Did she flush it down with her improperly working cistern?

I didn't know why I had not lost my attraction for this girl.

The only thing I knew was—she was a Comet. I stood there for a few minutes, reviving how we had reached here.

This was the same girl who happily kissed, hugged, and held my hand as I emerged from the Arc de TRIOMF metro two days ago.

What did I do to change her mind?

***

A vast crowd holding slogans against Russia stood in the middle of that mighty monument, who awaited a peaceful return to their motherland. The black banner looked gibberish to me, though I could understand the emotions they were going through. My beautiful Ukrainian girl was also one of those people with the black banner.

"I will be late by five minutes."

The devil's gadget smiled once again when it delivered a message from her like a pigeon.

I continued my support for the Ukrainians by photographing and posting on social media, which was an obvious way to make a statement during that period.

Followed by the message. I smiled back at the devil's gadget and took off to the entrance of the metro station, waiting for her.

A few moments later, she appeared before me, spreading her scent across the Arc de TRIOMF. We kissed, intertwined fingers, and walked towards the Ciutadella Parc, as usual.

The park was lush green and windy. People walked with their beautiful dogs, both big and small—the only animals who loved back without any expectations but with a lot of anxiety. Some people rode their scooters and bikes through the crowd. A few children and elders fed the parrots and the pigeons. A queue extended to the entrance of the park for boating in the small pool that was placed precisely in the centre of that place.

Before I could enjoy a moment of that eternal beauty, my heart pondered around the upcoming days and how I would miss her.

"Miss, I have a surprise for you at home." I said.

"What is it, tell me?"

"No, you have to come and see by yourself."

"I can't come today; I must return home after the Ukrainian protest. I have a road trip with my friends tomorrow. Day after tomorrow, let's have a brunch together and then I want to chill at home" she completed everything in a single breath.

I didn't know what chill meant. The drawback of not being a native English speaker was that, I had yet to become familiar with many slangs, idioms, and phrases. My emotionality erupted without waiting to realize what she meant, and I ignored the words *brunch together* in between her statements.

"See, I will be in Andorra next weekend. After that, I will be in Munich for a week, and you will be in Mallorca. We can't meet for another three weeks" I got upset.

The eruption did not suffice.

"I fixed my bed and bought a new blanket in your favourite colour, purple and bought a pair of new slippers for you because you needed them there."

She did not let me complete, "stop, this is breaking all the limits. Oh my god! You are not giving me the breathing space. Don't you want to sit here and enjoy the beauty?"

"Yes, I am emotional. Doing things for you means I like you so much. Perhaps I love you, which I am not yet ready to say." I didn't answer her question about enjoying the beauty of that scenic park. Instead, the emotional uproar continued resembling those who paraded on the other end of that park, shouting for their motherland.

We both stood up from the bench we were sitting on and started walking towards the protest location without speaking much. The eruption stopped when I came back to my senses.

What just happened?

"Sorry! I got a little upset because I will miss you." I told her with my softest of expressions.

"I told you we could have brunch and be together on Sunday. Every time this happens, I'm sorry, but I don't think this is working anymore. I need to be myself. I need my space. I can't breathe."

Her voice broke like someone who was struggling to breathe while she said that.

I was intruding too much into her private space; we had only been seeing each other for a month. The questions about what happened were not necessary anymore. She also sounded needy at times, and she mentioned it, too—maybe just once or twice.

"Did I just ruin it?" I introspected.

The rest of the day passed on more in silence. All left for the day were the Ukrainian slogans against Russians and the war.

*"Slava Ukraini, Heroyam Slava[10]"*

A cold goodbye notified the summons to underline the end of that relationship with a red line. When I thought the time would heal my emotional drama, it didn't.

The next day morning, once again, the devil's gadget came into play.

*Good morning, ma majesty! Have a great trip.*

*Hey, you can plan your Sunday on your own. Your emotionality is too much for me*, she replied.

The devil made me write a dozen messages back, spamming her inbox and mind beyond repair.

And then—The ghost mode started.

# VI

# The Realization

My anxiety often consumed me, leaving me feel like a clown stumbling and falling from his trapeze, repeatedly plummeting into a safety net. Having such safety nets in the form of supportive shoulders was undeniably crucial in life, guiding us forward when we feel stuck. Though there weren't many shoulders for me to lean on, there were a couple of them. strong enough to hold me without causing my tears to overflow like a burst dam. My heart felt as if a massive hammer had shattered it, each piece reflecting my pain like scenes from a poignant Indian movie set to a sad song, emphasizing the agony of lost love.

"Vasi, bro."

My eyes were filled. He was not there to give me advice but to console me to face it.

"Bro, life has to move on," Vasi said

"Not for everyone, my friend." My Greek friend smiled at that answer with twinkling eyes.

"I know how you feel"

Yes, he did know.

"It was my mistake. I can't forgive myself ever for this."

He offered me a glass of vermouth and some pizza. My brain didn't want to eat much; however, my body was relentlessly striving to eat something for a stomach that had kept empty the past 24 hrs. I was tired and pissed.

I re-invented my friendship with the long tube filled with tobacco and my stomach filled with beers.

"Do you think one month was enough to unlearn 20 years of romance?

She was unique and exceptional. She was not just another star you see every night.

She was a comet." I continued.

"In the past few hours that I spent alone in a museum, it only depicted me more as a ruin from an archaeological site without clearing my mind."

"Woh woh!! Too much man. You will find someone else. There are millions of other comets on this universe. It's just that this time needs to pass on, too." Vasi stopped me abruptly.

"Someone else huh! A star perhaps. Not a comet. Unfortunately, Jophiel, the comet, has lost its attraction to this creature on Earth, apparently it can never be revived. I wish if I had a time machine"

I smirked with the look of a hangdog completing my statement

"Maybe she is scared of relationships?" said Vasi.

"Maybe, maybe not. But I am sure she will move on quickly. I am emotionally intense due to my past. I overdid things to ensure that I didn't lose this time, and I just did because of that. Whatever! It's late. We need to work tomorrow, right?" I finished my dialogue with a painful smile.

We lit another cigarette in the wet balcony of Vasi's apartment.

It was raining cats and dogs. The weather reckoned how I felt—rain followed by snow in the mountains. I wondered if she was also feeling the same. She might be emotionally intense. I might have pushed her away, but she was still a human who cries, gets angry, and laughs out loud.

After a lot of kisses from Mausi, the anxious dog from the streets of Greece; I left Vasi's apartment at Bac de Roda, fully drenching in rain. Instead of walking towards my house, I went precisely in the opposite direction to reach Encants. I stood in front of the massive door of her apartment that we opened together many times—like a stalker. I lit a cigarette which became wet in those heavy drizzles before burning out. I befriended the next one that burnt empty too soon as well. I strolled towards the Encants station crushing the empty cigarette packet as hard as possible before dumping it in the trash can.

"Okay, Guru,"

I turned around in a flash to see no one around.

Guru—a call that I often heard hilariously from her mouth while commenting on my debates on politics, science, or literature. This time, it was just the alcohol playing games with me.

I reached home quite late, wet and freezing. But it seemed as if nothing had happened to my body.

Did I sleep that day? The next day? Or the next?

I was relying on my oldest friends: a book and a pen.

I wrote my first line – "Destroy the Devil's gadget."

# VII

# The Hope

The beautiful dawn greeted me with its gentle breeze and the soft melody of birds, filling the small world around me. Usually, I would have loitered lazily indoors at those hours, but today felt different. Today, I felt compelled to step out and embrace the quiet beauty of the morning.

As I ventured outside, the drizzle in La Pau mirrored the gentle recovery of my mind. Each droplet seemed to echo the lesser melancholy of my thoughts, falling softly like whispers of introspection.

"Hola!" My neighbour, who was out with his best friend, shouted out loud.

I walked closer to him

"Seems too early for you, isn't it?" He asked

He knew neither my name nor I knew his, but Blume—his friend— started jumping over me. I bent down, cuddled, and kissed him like always.

"Quite early for me today. Seems like I had insomnia last night." I smirked, and then we laughed together.

"Bye"

"Adios"

We used our best languages and departed

I took out the devil's gadget and played a song.

*Feeling groovy*...The 69th Street Bridge song by Simon & Garfunkel.

"Isn't that 59th street?? Aah! Never mind," I soliloquized and kept walking towards Encants.

During my evening walks, an old couple who always smiled at me at the Bac de Roda Park, were there that morning too. They sat at the same bench giving me a wonderful smile of contentment.

"Don't they sleep? How many years have they been together? Should be at least 3–4 decades."

As usual, I smiled back and continued my trail.

By the time I reached Encants, it was dry enough, reminding me that her heart had been deserted and that she might have moved on already.

Would she be thinking about me, at least for a moment? I last used the devil's gadget a day and a half ago to text her.

What if she wanted to see me? Or what if she felt different if we spoke or saw each other just over a coffee or walk?

I always thought, *bake when the oven was still hot.*

It could be one of the worst theories I learned in life. People could be like shadows; the closer the light reaches them, the faster they diminish.

A series of doubts kept popping up inside me. Would she discuss this with her friends? What would they say?

Cultural difference.

Toxic.

Identify the incompatibility.

Or what would her books say?

Avoidance

Anxious

Secure

Was I too emotional?

Whatever, I was depressed. I chuckled at myself. I was emotional, and I was overly trying to please her, make her happy, and be the best. But what if she was still in the avoidance zone and scared of relationships?

Relationships cannot be built without emotions; if there were hearts involved, there would be heartbreaks as well.

All I had to do was just be myself.

Now that the train had passed the station, all I could have done was to catch it at the next station or wait for the next one.

But I was ready to walk back home as another train might be able to take me to my destination.

Still, I always took the purple line even though I had to walk a long way to my office expecting to see her somewhere in the metro or the stations; to have accidentally bumped into her; for an opportunity to win her back and lose her never again; to affectionately display the better of me.

The question remained, if she would be brave enough to try again or give up without a fight.

I would have fought to flourish it into a beautiful relationship. Her side of the story really didn't matter anymore. It was, what it was! Once I had that mindset, I was only slightly bothered.

However, she was not just a Comet!

She was a piece of Art!!

She was a Poem!!!

Indeed, those were the decades that happened for me in weeks.

Life is a very fierce master in which exams are given first, and then the lessons followed. Some realizations come late because relationships start when we find perfections among the imperfections.

Back home, after a shower and my daily workout, I dressed in my favourite dark maroon shirt and dropped a gum in my mouth.

Keys, sunglasses, laptop and I was ready for office.

I put on my headphones walking towards the metro station to catch my L2 that passes through Encants.

The headphones played,

"Life I love you, always groovy…"

***

## Beginning of the end

"And then the frame zooms out on him standing on Passeig de Gracia L2 metro station by the yellow pillar near the vending machine where they kissed on the first date." Manel closed the script file.

For a moment, everything looked still. Manel's heart pounded with questions, emotions, and hopes.

Hannah's eyes were filled with tears.

"Let's shoot this here in Barcelona; I don't think any other city in the world can speak about such a story. True cosmopolitan and emotionally attached."

She said in a trembling voice.

"Can so many emotions arise in a month of dating?" asked Dan, with pity in his question.

"Come on Dan. Romeo and Juliet happened in five days." Manel giggled and continued. "I am planning to meet the guy this weekend for any additions or deductions."

"No, Manel. We don't need any amendments. It should go as it is. You find the best names, but far from reality, and change the locations if they are real, too,"

Hannah responded in a Victorian commanding style.

"It is time for us to leave; I don't want to miss the flight. I have a comet waiting for me in LA." Dan tried to soften the mood.

"For the movie's name – I think 'The Ukrainian Girl' might suit," Manel said.

Hannah and Dan stood up from the chair. Hannah wore her black winter coat, which was sleeping cosily in the next chair, and said,

"No Manel, I meant the name of the characters"

They walked towards the door of Star Bucks, where their taxi awaited. Manel stood in his land, proudly thinking about his first movie as a director.

"Good luck; that was a nice one. Let's give the industry an unfinished love story." Dan hugged him, moved towards the cab, and said, "Bye, man."

Hannah greeted Manel with the typical Spanish kisses and said,

"Let me discuss this further and my secretary will be in touch with you to discuss the dates and other stuff. We need to start casting ASAP if we need to do this.

See you soon."

As the black limo cab got ready to whisk away into the bustling Barcelona city centre, drowning in the cacophony of urban sounds, Hannah leaned out of the window and declared in a voice that rose above that chaos,

"Manel, Let's name it—She is a Poem!"

The cab vanished into the sea of vehicles, leaving those words hanging in the air.

Manel embarked on his solitary return journey with a mind throbbing with the dreams of his cinematic vision, whispering— "**She is a Poem**".

# A 'KEY' STORY

## A Summer Story

The haunting melody from my favourite television show on Netflix—Peaky Blinders, repeatedly played like a lullaby, transporting my thoughts to ramble around the gritty streets of Birmingham in the early 90's. It simulated me into a member of that youth urban gang like the enigmatic Tommy Shelby. I wandered in my dream through the alleyways and dimly lit corners of the old Birmingham. Rahul Shelby, my alter ego in dreams, effortlessly twirled his revolver with the finesse of the legend—gunslinger. Every spin of the gun brought me back to reality from a hallucination. I kept wondering why my arm was stretching to grab something else, only to realize the ringtone of my mobile phone. The strains of the Peaky Blinders theme continued to echo as a bridge between my fantasy and reality. It had been ringing for some time, but the trance did not let me return to the senses due to a tiring, sleepless night.

"It's only half past seven in the morning. Who the heck is calling so early?" I soliloquized.

Friday mornings typically unfolded at a leisurely pace, offering a harmony from the usual hustle and bustle of city life. For the Barcelona Street Dwaags, a group with camaraderie and shared experiences, Thursdays held a special significance. It was on these evenings that they would come together, embarking on adventures through the labyrinthine streets of Barcelona.

Their gatherings were not merely about running errands or checking off to-do lists; they were opportunities to explore the depths of human connection, nuances of love, and mutually agreed conjugations. The street dwaags navigated through the intricate dance of relationships, each step bringing them closer to a deeper understanding of modern society.

"I went to bed only at 2 O'clock this morning after a disastrously failed clubbing filled with disappointments, which was not an unexpected outcome of forced chemistries for many mischievous single men."

I once again whispered to myself with a grin on my face and picked up the phone that was screaming—*Take a little walk to the edge of town*[1].

"Hello Rahul, did you wake up, bro?" Rajeev asked in his husky little voice.

Even though he was calling from India, he was aware of the time zones as he had lived most of his life on this side of the world.

To our group of Indian colleagues who had found their acquaintances in Barcelona, Rajeev was much more than a friend. He assumed the role of a guiding figure, like an elder brother. This dynamic was not uncommon among members of our community, who often sought out connections with those who shared their *lengua materna* and cultural background. For us, it was a Dravidian language called Malayalam spoken by the people of Kerala—a south Indian state.

India was supposed to be categorized as a continent, not a country. At the same time, Kerala should be a country rather than a state whose richness in diversity would still be beyond that of a Schnitzel, Pizza or Tapas!

It was a tendency rooted in people to connect with those, who shared the same language and culture, to bridge the gap between the familiar and the unfamiliar in a foreign land..

"Hey! you woke me up now" I replied with a slight laugh that could be heard from the other end.

"Da! Something urgent! Since last night, Raj has not responded to his wife's calls and texts. Even I tried calling, and he has not!"

I could hear the depth of worry in Rajeev's voice, as if something was severely wrong.

"Don't worry! I'll head over to his place and see what's going on,"

I reassured him with a tone of empathy and hung up the call just before pulling the blanket over my face again.

"Come on! It's only half past seven; he should be sleeping. The mornings are still cold in Barcelona, shrinking even my penis to the smallest size like a snail inside its shell," I muttered to myself.

But my internal monologue was short-lived as Rahul Shelby resumed twirling his gun to the background score of Peaky Blinders again.

"Who the fuck is this now?" I muttered with an irritation that crept into my voice as I picked up the phone again, only to find Ragini on the other end—Raj's wife.

It was not even five minutes since I told Rajeev that I would go and check. I listened to Ragini's trembling voice, which quickly turned into sobs.

"Rahul! He hasn't picked up the call or texted me back since last night?" Her distress poured out as loud weeping through the phone. I dropped all thoughts of Shelbys and their guns, slipping on my Deerstalker hat. My senses heightened, adrenaline rushing through me as Mr. *Doyle's*[4] plot began to unfold in my sixth sense.

A series of questions followed as part of the detective interrogation.

Question 1: "When was the last time you spoke to him?"

Question 2: "Did you call both his phones?"

Question 3: "Do you usually call him this early?"

Question 4: "Did you…?"

She interrupted me, hindering my investigative skills.

Her answer came back quite swiftly, "Usually, I call him around seven O'clock in Spain to wake him up. But today, he has not picked up my call. You know, he's been dealing with some health issues recently."

Wow! I couldn't help but note her awareness of Central European Time—quite a leap for someone from the outskirts of Kerala, known as the God's own country.

God's own country was a phrase frequently used to describe Kerala, due to its lush greenery, natural elegance, and cultural richness. The origins of this term have been debated regularly due to its unclear interpretations.

Some argued that the region was cherished and protected by a divine force, making it a paradise on earth. Others interpreted it as a land filled with gods or divine beings—not the ones in mythological books, but the kind of Gods who were at the top of their caste chains, money chains, and power chains, ultimately making them the alphas of their food chains.

Ragini's second statement about health issues was quite atrocious! I couldn't find her concern misplaced. After all, the majority of the world's population struggles with health issues related to either undernourishment or over-nourishment. So, whatever she called health issues were caused by over-eating and lack of exercise—an over-nourishment state called obesity. They weren't the ones who ate just once a day when a significant portion of the global population failed to access sufficient nutritious meals at least once a day.

The investigation moved to the next level.

She continued, "I called the office and his personal phone; both are working and ringing, but there was no response. I spoke to him last night, and he was completely fine."

"Completely fine, presumably, fully functional?" I interrupted. Was that rude? Maybe, it was!

Whatever, it's not the time to perform a "Political correctness" test. She started weeping louder. OMG! A continuous eruption of empathy trekked through my neurons.

"Don't worry! I am going to his house now to check him out directly and will make a WhatsApp video call from there, with him"

"Okay, brother, please!" she replied without stopping to weep.

I looked at the time; It was almost 8' O clock.

Almost 8'O clock, exactly that's how we Indians say time.

Does that mean we don't value time? No. Not at all!

Sometimes, we could be late for an appointment by a few minutes, sometimes, rarely, maybe 65 or 70 minutes, but never above an hour. Otherwise, small increments like 5-10-15 minutes never sounded very critical to us. Nothing in this world would have changed during those minutes, wouldn't it?

Ragini was beyond such increments that day.

I wondered if their astrological competence was checked before ringing their wedding bells. Raj was a person with a great, unmatchable affinity towards "communism or a modified version of socialism" (Ssshh, something that cannot be heard loud in Europe). It was impossible that he could have checked *kundali*. Whatsoever! With or without the star alignment, their love life had been beaten up with a big test by the Universe on that specific day in the horoscope calendar.

I was passing through a point in my life where I proclaimed myself as an atheist and encouraged people not to accept the so-called universal supremacy - the uncle with a long white beard in the sky who created the world - lived in heaven - travelled through the clouds. He would be waiting for us at the gate of heaven and had a big book with the list of good and evil we did in our lives on this planet that he created. He decided if he had to fry people in a pan of oil or sent us near the river of wine with hot Latinas all around, based on the balance between those good and evil.

Before moving to the next level of this tale, the reality check emphasizes that Ragini's distress was obviously not due to the situation itself. At that juncture, she did not have the power to revoke her emotions without confirmation, and precisely, that's what she was looking for from me.

I finished brushing my teeth, an act that I performed once or twice every day, without fail and changed my attire to the weary denim and T-shirt from the night before. However, the real dilemma arose with the choice of perfume as I was still stinking from the night out.

Who cared? At that moment, the only thing that truly mattered was where on earth was Raj?

I rushed to catch a train from the La Pau metro station to Joanic, one of the longest journeys in L4 lane.

# I

# Train to Joanic

From La Pau to Joanic, there were approximately twenty stations, followed by a kilometre walk to Raj's house.

After that?

I was utterly clueless about how this adventure would unfold. No Shelbys or Sherlocks were there to join my rescue mission, so the notion of collecting as much intel as possible crept into my mind.

To my surprise, there he was – Mr Raheem, the Pakistani fellow who ran a salon in my neighbourhood where I visited regularly to get my haircut. Unfortunately, they never offered pedicure services, for that I had to walk another 500 meters down the road if I had to have one. That was precisely why my toes had never experienced the luxury of a Spanish pedicure. I often wondered what kind of operation he was running there apart from the salon. Most evenings, as I stroll past the *perruqueria*[6], I spy on a woman tucked away in a corner, diligently crunching numbers or something, which aroused my curiosity. So far, there haven't been enough clues to crack that case, but now's my chance to strike up a chatty tête-à-tête with Mr. RP.

"Oh! Rahul bhai, where to, so early in the morning?" Mr. RP asked.

"Brother, Salaam! (good day) One of my friends has not responded to his wife since last night, and we cannot reach him on his mobile phone either. He had some health issues as well. His wife was so worried and called me early this morning. Now I am going to his place to check his status."

"Allah ka Shukr (With God's grace)! Don't worry! Nothing bad will happen. Allah! Will take care of everything!"

"Brother, is there any emergency number to contact in Barcelona, if I need."

"Google it! Brother. You will get it easily. Allah! Will take care"

When did Google have Allah's direct phone number?

"Alright, brother. I will Google it in case of an emergency. I hope nothing is bad," I smirked while stressing the word Google.

Mr RP took a big sigh and repeated, "Allah will take care of everything."

"It's my stop." Mr RP shook my hands and tapped my shoulders like in old Bollywood movies, as if I were mourning somebody's death. The only piece missing in that conversation was a sad song with beautiful girls in their colourful attire dancing in the background.

*Take a little walk to the edge of town.*

I picked up the call. It was Ragini again.

"I will reach in 25 minutes and then call you from there. Everything will be fine, don't be upset.

I hung up the call without waiting to hear the rhapsody of missing her husband.

Given my limited knowledge of the legal matter, even the police will only register a missing adult case after 12–15 hours.

They should've definitely consulted Kundali! I meant, who knew if it was already written in the stars, etched into their palms, or whispered in their weekly horoscope, waiting to give them the much-needed peace of mind? *Kundali*[5] was like the Swiss Army knife of life—it could help you tie the knot, untie it (yikes!), or even use in the marital boat in case of dowry concerns.

And let's not forget the absolute deal-breakers: being *maanglik* or having *chovva dosham* can even sabotage a relationship! Apparently, having these cosmic red flags could not only prevent you from walking down the aisle but also put your future spouse in some serious peril. Who knew astrology was so lethal?

But wait, there's more! Kundali didn't stop at marital matters; it also had a detailed roadmap for your entire family tree. It could forecast the exact number of kids, spouses, parents, siblings or—you name it!

So, all that relationship emotional trauma, anxiety, and tension? Turns out, it was all for nothing! If only they had just checked their astrological forecast, they could've saved themselves a whole lot of stress and even a few therapy bills!

*Take a little walk to the edge of town*

5 minutes later—Ragini called again

"I will reach there in 20 minutes and call you. Everything will be fine; don't get upset." I repeated my statement more empathetically, adjusting just the duration of my trip before hanging up the call.

*Take a little walk to the edge of town*

Ten minutes later—Ragini repeated.

"I will be there in fifteen minutes and call you. Everything will be fine; don't get upset," I repeated more empathetically, adjusting the time.

This process continued every five minutes until I reached the Joanic station.

Same Ragini, same sobbing, same statements. It even made me think of an automatic response in my mobile for her calls as;

*I will reach Raj's house in T-25 minutes, after which I will make a WhatsApp video call with him, from his house. Everything will be fine; please don't be upset, please be patient and wait for my call.*

I also wondered if I was confused about the time zones. Indian Standard Time might have started moving faster than Central European Standard Time. Since my knowledge of geography and time was decent, I intended to refrain from performing further scrutiny in this area, at least for the time being.

The devil's gadget rang again. Ragini, it was—who else could it be! "I am walking towards the house now," I said.

"You said that you will reach in twenty-five minutes?" Ragini responded just like she was ready for an ambush.

"Meri ma, I told you that I would reach the station in twenty-five minutes. Don't worry, I will call you as soon as I reach home?" I responded peacefully, remembering her state of mind.

(*Meri ma* is an Indian slang that's used with women when people are fed up with something. In an ideal world, it meant—my mom)

Unexpectedly, there was an overlapping call.

"Ragini, I am getting an urgent call, maybe a lead. I will call you back right after."

I didn't wait for her response and hung up immediately.

It was Rodrigues, the local Spanish guy from Barcelona who worked with Raj. The last living soul I know of, who had seen Raj alive, right before he left the office. Rodrigues responded to some of the questions I raised through chat while on the train.

"Hey! Ra(h)ul, what (h)appened?"

The Spanish people usually hate the sound" h," especially when it's used as 'h' at the beginning of a word. The only letter in the alphabet I know of in Spanish that gives a purpose to 'h' is 'c' with words like *chicos* and *chao*. However, they love using 'h' when replaced with 'j'. They should officially consider removing the letter" h" from their alphabet to avoid such "chaos" in the language.

I lived in Europe for a few years already to realize that English was not a global language anymore, despite what the Britishers used to boast. My education from a commonwealth country with the dominance of English never taught me that I would still need help with my survival instincts in this part of the world. In India, people who speak English were considered elite class, however, it wasn't going to change the fact in Spain.

"Hey, Rody, Raj had not responded since last evening. Was he okay when he left the office last evening? I meant health-wise?"

"Yeah, (h)e was fine! What [h]appened now?"

"No idea. I am on my way to his house; I will let you know if I have any news," I emphasized.

"Sure, please let me know!" Rody hung up.

I heard of different definitions for *a fraction of second.* In India, we believed that it was the time taken by the vehicle right behind you to honk at you, as soon as a traffic signal turned green—irrespective of how far your vehicle stood from the signal.

But that day, Ragini took the time to dial my number after I hung up the previous call.

This time, I picked up the phone with a different response.

"Don't disconnect the call, I am almost there." I told Ragini.

The "almost" here means it would take five more minutes to walk up the hill towards Parc Guell to reach Raj's apartment.

After a few signals and crossings, I reached his apartment's front gate, carrying Ragini in my hand and my phone.

"What is the apartment number Ragini?" I asked her since I couldn't recollect it instantly.

"Bro, it is 2B."

I decided to press the bell button, and then she appeared. A lady in her late thirties, gorgeous, well-mannered, and well-dressed, even in her home attire—precisely, pyjamas.

She asked me quite a few things in Espanol or Catalan, but my linguistic skills did not help me to distinguish between them.

All I understood was, "compañero Raj?"

"Si – Como es el?"

"*Da*[2]!" Before she answered, Raj gave a loud shout from far in his friendly mother tongue slang.

He appeared as the reincarnation of the blue God, Lord Vishnu, from Hindu mythology.

The blue God had Sudharshana chakra—a weapon that was used to kill the asuras in one hand and a pure white sea shell on the other. Asuras were big black men who were often considered demons or evil. The white sea shell was intended to announce victory over the black asuras.

This perfectly aligned with the Indian stereotype of black and white ethnicity. We always required a person with a fair complexion, to dance in the centre of a group, marry, host huge events, to play the lead character in a movie, in fashion ramps—predominantly advertisements and many other *auspicious* occasions. People with darker complexion were seen mostly selling vegetables, cleaning roads or doing other petty jobs.

On this instance, Raj replaced the chakra and the sea shell with a long broom and a dustpan. Of course, he looked like the reincarnation of Lord Vishnu. However, as I walked closer, his resemblance apparently became more similar to the Prime Minister of India. The PM who habitually posed in front of the media with a broom and a dustpan on the cleanest roads.

I looked around. To my disappointment, no paparazzi were spotted.

I turned Ragini's voice into visuals in that WhatsApp call.

"Raj Etta."

Etta—a colloquial word in Malayalam that was equally versatile as the word fuck in English. When fuck could be used as a noun, pronoun, adjective, adverb, etc., Etta could be used to call anyone in this world irrespective of their age, relationship, or nationality; only respect matters.

Ragini screamed excitedly like a 3-year-old child who saw her favourite chocolate in her father's hands. Raj ran up the stairs like a Bollywood hero at the start of a romantic song. He grabbed my phone in no time. Ragini's sobbing turned into laughter as if her daddy had already given her the chocolate. I moved to the other side to better understand the 'lady in pyjamas.'

# II

# The Smelly Kitchen Dustbins & Keys

The emotional drama did not last long. The call was disconnected, triggering Ragini to return to her forgotten households. My flirting with the lady in pyjamas could have worked more efficiently due to her proficiency in English and mine in Spanish. Time travelling worked precisely, as explained by Stephen Hawkins and Albert Einstein through the narratives of Raj. He also ensured that every vocabulary and sentences were 'politically correct.'

"Rahul, come down"

I followed Raj to his apartment with his landlord – the lady in pyjamas.

In the alleyway leading to his apartment's main door, I stumbled upon an old man attempting to break the lock using an array of tools—a chisel, hammer, electric cutter, screwdriver, driller, and whatnot. As we approached, the man launched into a rapid-fire stream of Spanish, incomprehensible to my ears except for the unmistakable message: get out of his workspace, pronto.

Didn't he sound a tad rude? No surprise there. I could picture Raj, with his zero experience in lock-picking but a surplus of micromanagement skills, trying to lend a hand earlier. When I walked down together with Raj, for the man with the hammer, it must have seemed like a classic case of two managers attempting to solve a problem with a single resource. A scenario all too familiar in the corporate world. Since my Espanol is *poquito*[7] better than Raj, I pulled him out of the place towards the lawn before the man turned into a ripper.

As the bright sun beamed down on Barcelona, Raj launched into his account of the break-in with his signature casual tone.

"Last night, I got back from the office pretty late," he started, his demeanour as subtle as ever.

Typical workaholic, I thought to myself. No doubt his late-night arrival was just another day in Raj's life.

"As soon as I stepped inside, I remembered I had to take out the trash," Raj said.

I just nodded my head in the typical Indian way.

Raj's apartment was a bachelor's paradise, with a spacious kitchen, grey furniture, white-painted walls, and a huge television in the living room. In his sincere efforts to support the authorities and keep the environment intact, he always diligently sorted his waste and ensured it was disposed of properly—a stark contrast to mine.

With his eyes wide behind his thick spectacles, Raj launched into the next part of his story. His gaze was so intense that, it seemed like, his eyes behind those glasses might fly off his face like rogue eggs.

"When I entered, I put the key in the keyhole and opened it." He began, only to meet my sarcastic interruption.

"Of course, that's how we all open doors," I jested, unable to resist the opportunity for a playful jab.

Raj shot me a disapproving look and a dialogue before continuing his story, determined to stay on track despite my antics.

"You need to improve your listening skills. You're always like this, never let others finish,"

I chuckled. But I wasn't about to let him stray from the topic.

"Wait, wait, wait! Don't deviate. Then what happened?" I interrupted, eager to hear the rest of the story.

With a sigh, Raj resumed his narrative, his tone tinged with frustration.

"Okay, fine. When I entered, I put the key in the keyhole and opened it," he repeated, emphasizing each word. "Once inside, I took the key and inserted it in the keyhole inside the house."

His eyes wide behind his thick spectacles once again felt as if they might pop out and roll away.

"In the same door?" I questioned sceptically, unable to contain my doubt.

Raj nodded seriously. "Yes, the same door."

After a pitch of silence, during which I wondered why the hell someone would do that, he continued.

"Then I arranged the bins, separated them, and came out with them, leaving the keys inside the door. Only after shutting the door, I realized that the keys were inside."

Oh! Whattah puzzle. It should be added to the civil service examination question papers to find the candidates' analytical skills and logical reasoning. I sighed.

"Then I called Remi (the pyjama lady) for the rescue. But we could not open the door from outside because we didn't have a spare key. We would not have been able to open it even if we had a spare key since the other one was already stuck from inside."

"But did you try that already? Are you sure?" I frowned. It brought in another dozens of questions in my mind.

"By the way, I know an alternate story about a safe house for your key."

"Yeah, there is one with Rejith" – Raj answered

"Why didn't you call him and try with the alternate key?" I asked.

"Yes, buddy, I gave him spare keys to manage such situations, but both my phones were inside."

"Okay, then you should have called from Remi's phone."

"I don't know his mobile number by heart."

"Okay, then you should have called Ragini. I hope at least you know her's by heart. You could have then asked her to reach out to one of us to organize the spare key. Also, she would be aware of the situation, which could have eased her tension this morning."

You should probably call Rejith to arrange the keys in the keychain—in order, right?"

I closed my topic with sarcasm.

Raj took a deep breath.

"Where were your phones?" I continued showering Raj with the arrows of questions.

"They were also inside, I told you." An embarrassed smile followed from Raj.

It was time for me to stop showering the arrows of question. Otherwise, it would have led Raj to rest in the bed of arrows like the

*Pitamahan*[9], who watched the whole *Kurukshetra*[8] war of Mahabharata—the biggest epic from India, in a bed of arrows because of his particular boon to die only when he wanted. Unfortunately, Raj did not have any such boons, and it was not the time for him to rest. He was obliged to watch the war that the old man was fighting with his door due to his imprudence.

Suddenly, my *deerstalker*[3] cap kicked in again...

"Where did you sleep then?"

"Remi arranged a room for me in her apartment to sleep."

"Ooh!" I exclaimed.

Those unfamiliar with that specific "Ooh" expression should understand its versatility in India. It can be used to express pain, sorrow, surprise, embarrassment, telling secrets, keeping secrets, not believing, for believing, hatred, vengeance, happiness, jealousy, envy, appreciation etc. etc., etc.

"Come, let's go for a coffee." Raj ignored the ongoing discussion without any intention of responding to my ooh.

Raj might not have eaten or drunk anything since last night, or perhaps he simply didn't want to delve into the sleepover topic any further. After some coaxing, I agreed to grab a quick breakfast at the nearest 365—a famous coffee shop chain in the city. The topics on our way to 365 had taken curious turns, moving from Remi to the door, the lock, the break-in, and even entering into the politics of Kerala. It was just as, we were following a winding path through a maze of topics, with each turn leading us somewhere unexpected.

On our way back, we spotted Remi walking her mother to the nearest medical centre. She waved excitedly at us, and he waved back with equal enthusiasm that did not distract us even momentarily from the bizarre events of the morning.

Upon returning home, to our utter surprise, we found that the old man had somehow managed to gain entry into the house. Apparently, he had unscrewed the kitchen windows to get inside, instead of the front door, which he was trying to break open. The front door was left to suffer with numerous drill holes and a disastrously burned lock, but it was still locked.

I didn't feel like blaming the old man's efforts to break the door if sneaking in through the windows after removing a few screws were an option that did not appear early.

Sometimes, things work out differently than we predict. Accepting the unpredicted is not *easy*, and *easy* does not come to the lives of grownups *easily*.

Raj's micro-managerial skills were boosted by mixed emotions.

*Happiness*—the front door, even though torn apart, was wide open with the keys from inside.

*Deep sorrow*—Now he had to pay for repairing the door and also the windows, including labour charges for both.

*Anxiety*—How much would the insurance company pay back?

*Potential orgasms*—Both the phones were back in hand.

We went inside the house, and I grabbed a Turia beer from his refrigerator without asking his permission; at least he owed me that. Raj called his sole love, Ragini, once again to update her on the final status of that significant outage.

Until the beer was over, we once again discussed numerous variables under the sky and beyond outer space, like Christopher Nolan and Steven Spielberg. In between, Raj also spoke about developing a modus operandi to manage the keys better beyond his current backup plans.

A backup plan for a backup plan.

My instincts told me that, he would once again call Rejith to re-arrange the keys in his key chain.

Ragini never called again to my phone, and with sleepy eyes, I started my voyage back to the L4 Joanic metro station towards La Pau.

My deerstalker cap kept questioning several other possibilities, which could open the doors for many more stories, such as,

Why did Raj put the key in the door from the anterior keyhole?

Why didn't he attempt to reach Rejith once, even when they had no spare keys to test?

Why didn't he inform Ragini last night itself?

Isn't Remi quite attractive and seductive?
What if? —

Quite a lot of 'what ifs?' crossed my mind in a series.

Like quantum physics orates, everyone sees different truths because everyone creates what they see.

I giggled at myself for my naughty thoughts. I leaned against the door of the metro; my sleepy eyes anticipated the incident to be recreated in a spicier way in my forthcoming dreams. It was as if, reality had taken on a surreal twist, leaving me to ponder the fanciful nature of perception and experience.

# THE EPIC OF HOPE

## A Spring Story

proliferation of mould had tunnelled its way around the corners of his living room, shrouding the entire ceiling. A grim reminder of the hopelessness that had seeped into his life. Sitting on the dull grey sofa all day, his gaze fixed upon the spreading mould. Nothing seemed to be going right for him in the city of dreams yet.

Did they call this city, *the city of dreams* because you get to dream enough here, or was that for the number of dreams it could eventually fulfil? More precisely, would that be the aspirations it inspired, or was it merely a place where the dreams eventually withered away?

Loneliness encased him like the frost of winter, mirroring the solitary glass of water on his table, offering nothing but a reflection of his lost love. An ethereal presence that once illuminated his life with boundless radiance; An archangel who lived in another side of the planet and now vanished.

Choosing to end one's own life in the heat of battle would undoubtedly be the height of folly. It would not only betray your courage but also disregard the potential impact on loved ones left behind. The shadows cast by despair and hopelessness might appear large, but succumbing to them would only prolong a cycle of darkness.

The word 'coward' echoed in his mind like the resonant chimes of temple bells that flooded back his childhood memories.

Days with friends beneath the banyan tree's canopy, surrounded by the scent of turmeric, milk, and coconut oil. Those who sought solace and strength in the presence of *sarpams*[1] (the Hindu snake sculptures) adorned with offerings. It was here, amongst prayers and shared dreams, that they found the will to navigate life's challenges. For many, faith was a source of guidance through the darkest times.

Like someone said, irrespective of what science says, faith in God could never be a mistake if it could provide you with the strength you require to live a fulfilling life. If that's the case, would there be a need to reject the Big Bang theory, the origin of species, the organic or the inorganic evolution, the theories of embryological evolution, or other scientific facts?

The ultimate goal in life should be the attainment of peace and happiness. *God's existence or non-existence* should not be a hindrance to that. Believing or not would be no more than a personal choice. At the same time, the idea of each one's idolization should end at the tip of their nose, after that it's someone else's space.

The momentary thoughts made him drop the *Gillette*[2] blade—once a famous brand for a clean shave in India, but these days more associated with tearing veins and bleeding to death.

Suddenly, the devil's gadget played his favourite background score from Rocky Balboa to wake him up from the euphoria of death wishes.

*Ta-da tang. Ta-da taang*… Not sure if you could fantasise this music, recalling Sylvester Stallone running up the stairs towards the Philadelphia Museum of Art in his jogger's rig.

It kept ringing with a name on the screen that provoked him to pick up the phone instead of the blade.

"Hari! What's up!"

The mobile read the caller's name as Liz.

What the mobile did not know was the inventiveness behind the name that appeared on its screen, which had to be read as Elizaveta Goriachek. A Ukrainian girl who always said that she hated Russia today more than yesterday, but less than tomorrow.

Moving away from the word 'hatred' was the first thing he needed today.

"Liz, how come you called?" he giggled.

He sounded dramatic. He was about to cut his left hand's vein. This might be the so-called presence of God for believers, but for others—a mere coincidence.

"Do you want to come with me to Catalunya? I have some shopping before I go to London on vacation to meet my brother and parents."

"Really!" Hari replied sarcastically.

He always wondered about her shopping spree, which ended with *I, my,* and *mine.*

"Okay! Shall we meet in the square in an hour?"

"Yep, I will be there." He hung up.

The Gillette blade continued at its favourite place on the table, thirsty for blood, like the *emperor of Transylvania*[3], who maintained his youth by drinking blood, siempre. It was astonishing to discover why he drank blood, as it contained a whole universe of pathogens that could cause HIV, Hepatitis, Malaria, or even diabetes. Why did those things in the blood never impact his youthfulness? However, Hari's Romanian friends always denied the presence of such a blood drinker in their country. Ironically, they had not seen even a mosquito until they left their country.

Eventhough daylight savings had already started and the winter never left the doorsteps, he continued to enjoy standing under the hot shower for a prolonged period, though today, the shower time reduced to half. The smell of the cocoa butter lotion he spread over his torso made him feel rejuvenated. He should have applied this more often whenever he was down, as it gave him a pleasant sense of hope, which put him afar from reality. The selection of outfits felt like it was the next big decision in life: black, white, purple, grey, or more—black seemed more appropriate, reflecting his emotions of loss, despair, and regret. The tight black tees exhibited his pumped up, toned body, showing off the effort he put up every day at the gym.

Gym was a place where more singles hit throughout the day, to make themselves relieved from the stories that engraved their emotional status, and perchance to find a replacement partner. The scenes from gym often reminded the peacocks who danced, spreading their feathers, to attract a *better* opposite sex. It accurately endorsed the meaning of *better* as per the English dictionary.

Black tees and blue denim with a few accessories; once he locked the apartment and walked, his alter ego with zero joy was also left locked inside the door. He wore a fake smile that projected himself as a peaceful, happy, contended, and successful alpha male, who pretended to be a sigma since the beginning of winter.

The thoughts about beta, gamma, or delta never crossed his mind. Do they actually exist?

Curiosity drove the human race to where we arrived lately. But the curious humans kept commenting about such male dominations in this patriarchal world through Facebook, Instagram, and Twitter (now they call it by a different name, an 'X').

The deep thought for the evening was interrupted by a voice that came through the PA system of the train, which said, *Proxima Estacio Catalunya.*

"Liz! I am right in front of El Corte Ingles."

"Hey! I will be there in a minute." Liz hung up the phone without waiting for my answer.

He very well understood what a minute meant. Hari looked at his mobile; it was nineteen degrees Celsius that day; however, the sun was scorching with its brightness and warmth, making him feel more like twenty-nine degrees Celsius. It was probably not early spring but early summer, as if the globe had already wanted to skip the weather.

At a distance, a vast crowd was feeding the pigeons right in the middle of the Catalunya square, not because they wanted to. The actual intention was more towards making a few astounding photographs on their mobile phones. Long gone were the days when people walked up there with SLR cameras or automatic ones to take pictures, which were then washed in the darkroom or printed them with the help of a photo studio. There used to be a lot of locals who made their living by taking pictures of the tourists. They became an endangered species and were not visible much.

Nowadays, everyone has a mobile phone to take instant photographs without hassle. The tiny gadget can do anything—photos, videos, editing, morphing, AI beautification, and more. No wonder everyone looks fantastic in their photographs, with thinner bodies, clearer skins, and attractive backgrounds.

A kid around two or three was running around the pigeons and trying to kick them like a football. None seemed to care because the pigeons did not look frightened. Instead, the pigeons just jumped out of their way.

Tourism was picking up as the winter was already over. I was quite curious to know if this was actually true. You see people in Barcelona throughout the year, especially in this part of the city. The plausible reason for this crowd could be, the pigeons would have taken an extended vacation in the winter before they returned in spring.

"Hari"

He got startled and turned around. Stood right behind him was Liz— a beautiful girl of five feet and a few inches with lips that resembled hearts on playing cards, a sharp chin that repeatedly insisted on her independence, and loud laughter like the chime of a small bell that was spread around without consciousness.

"What plans?"

Hari asked instantly after Liz's tight hug, before she could become intuitive about the Gillette on his table.

"I want to go to Sephora and then Parfois to pick up a bag for my mom. After that, we can grab something, if you want, at your favourite L' Ovella Negra."

She finished the entire statement in a single breath.

The French Sephora, Portuguese Parfois, and Catalan L' Ovella Negra—real cosmopolitan world! Per se, *Walk of Shame*[4] was purposely ignored, he guessed.

"Come on, let's go!"

She didn't wait for his response and started walking towards Sephora, knocking out every tourist loosely walking through the pavements with the skill of a mature boxer, while holding Hari's hand like pulling a cow by its rope.

"Wooh! Hooh!"

She definitely wanted to avoid taking the escalator or the stairs, but the slide. She pushed him into the slide and followed instantly with her loud exclamations.

On the other hand, he was inexplicably unhappy to have missed the rituals of the escalators, which reminded him about the kisses, breath, and saliva that were passed between couples while climbing up and down.

She continued her chatterbox, broadcasting events from the past few days, weeks, and months. The boss, the HR, the roommate, the ex-boyfriend, the latest Tinder guy, the nail art, the plans for vacation at Londres, etc., etc. His lazily wandering mind pretended that everything was heard and understood with rhythmic nods that resembled the nodding Buddha that brought luck.

After about half an hour in a warzone, she finally decided to make peace at the cash counter. Neither he saw nor asked what was bought; instead, he played a friend's role by remarking nothing but— "Nice choices!"

She continued walking towards the Parfois, visible from Sephora, without leaving the end of the rope tied to his neck.

But there was something preciously unforgettable for him; it was a reality check that, if she had not started holding the other end of that rope a few hours back, it would have been tied somewhere else. Eventually it would have detached him from this world forever.

Knowingly or unknowingly, she was always a selfless creature.

"What happened to you? Why are you so quiet?"

This was the second time she had startled him in the past hour.

Did she have a mind reader installed in her brain?

"Nah! Nothing serious!! Just some random thoughts."

He put his hands over her shoulder and walked like a football player who improved his commitment and participation on the field.

"What's next? Bags?"

"Yeah, Hari. One for my mom and another one for my sister-in-law."

"Fair enough!" He replied.

The next few minutes were spent exploring the seasoned animal skin inside the store. Hari used this time religiously by trying to flirt with a beautiful female staff member. made his mind a bit more juvenile than how we woke up that day.

"Wow! Excellent choices. Which one is for your mom?"

"No, dude, she won't like either one. So, I took one for my sis-in-law and the other for me."

"Expected," Hari giggled.

Liz punched his arm making a *woosh* sound of embarrassment and chuckled.

"L' Ovella Negra?"

"Si, Por favor!"

Next was another fifteen-minute walk filled with the same boss, HR, roommate, ex-boyfriend, latest Tinder guy, nail art, plans for a vacation in London, etc. This time, the passes between them were much better, until they stopped for a street-side performer who played,

*"I wonder how, I wonder why,*

*yesterday you told me about the blue, blue sky*

*and all that I can see*[5]*…"*

They looked at each other. Liz observed that Hari was not singing along with the performer. It was one of his favourites, the one he always preferred to perform in front of small friend groups and get-togethers. Her mind clearly read what he was going through. He had not been the guy she used to know.

The boss, HR, roommate, ex-boyfriend, latest Tinder guy, nail art, plans for a vacation in London, and everything else stopped for a while.

"You should go and meet her," she said.

# I

# The Penultimate Chapter of Drama

The end of an epic triggered by egos was what fumed in the air during those nights.

Some people seemed too good to be true. Often, they were doubted due to the intensity of truth. Being born alone and dying alone was considered the only reality of life. Even then, individuals were compelled to adhere to a social construct that dictated the experience of sorrow, disappointment, anger, frustration, anxiety, depression, heartbreak, success, failure, and illusion.

The ideal human existence on Earth should be prioritized, connecting the time between birth and death, with happiness and peace. Evidently, it was impossible to comment about other planets or life forms in this universe, or the multiverse because, on this blue planet, humans possessed the gift of mortality, which allowed us to appreciate life. However, it was influenced by a moral code established by media and society.

For Hari, it was the fear of making a wrong decision, but in the end, was he satisfied that he took it for himself?

Probably not!

The reminiscence of olden days filled with fun feels like mere day dreams that had never ended once. The nights terminated after five or six in the colder mornings of Barcelona; those gales had already passed the horizon of memories beyond the existence of reality. As someone had said, the first half of one's life would be character building and setting the context, whereas the second half would be an eventful climax with drama, emotions, actions, twists, and turns, in which the lone effort would be to try to avoid clichés. Hari's life was more or less near this climax juncture.

The prime question to be answered was, whose *appeal to pity fallacy* was it? Devi or Hari??

The consequences of his actions began to unravel, and he had to face them. Nothing he said would have changed her mind, and he felt the pain of losing his love of life.

Was that even an unforgivable mistake? But perspectives matter; that change from individual to individual.

She compared him to her ex, but he didn't have an answer. He accepted what he did and pleaded for her pity, even though he never accepted that it was a mistake. Did that make him less of a man? He was an advocate of feminism, in a world that flourished as a patriarchal one.

Like the end of civilization, it had to go through every stage to reach anarchy;

Denial

Retaliation

Negotiation

War

Anarchy

There was no respect for boundaries, privacies, or control. Romantic love could be considered an addiction that Hari was struggling to get rid of. The reality of human grudges, egos, jealousies, and temperament was that, they always grew with age like bad wine.

Everything started from here, the Doll House. The place that triggered the euphoria of loneliness, and ended the rhapsody of coitus

***

*

"Hari! What are you doing this evening around seven? I want you to experience something."

Will said with a wink. "Chicas?"

"Por favor!" Hari pretended as if he had been speaking Spanish for years. However, he knew how to survive as a small fish in this vast ocean. In his two months in Barcelona, it was one of the words he learned to use without fear.

"When?"

"I will call you my dear friend,"

Will replied with a decorative giggle.

The whole day, until the evening, went in the anxiety of what that experience would be. Then came Will's WhatsApp message with the location.

It took less than ten minutes for him to get ready in a form that could best attract a woman. He walked to the metro and a few stations later, he walked again, swiftly, to reach the location directed by Google maps to reach the building that read, Dollhouse.

Days have changed.

Back in the days, people used to communicate with each other to find or reach a specific location. Nowadays, the technology replaced real humans. It took people to anywhere they wanted. Eventually, it reduced a lot of human interactions. Hari recalled his youth in his town, where many relationships evolved with a small enquiry about a direction or a place; unforgettable, long bus and train journeys that earned new friends. But, mobile phones taught us to ignore the people who sat next to us for hours, even the family at our dinner tables.

It was seven o'clock already, the night began, but it was still as bright as a day. A unique phenomenon realised by Hari after reaching Spain. He lived in a country quite close to the equator for most of his life, where day and night were bright and dark.

The Dollhouse entrance was decorated with bulbs blinking in a pattern that called him repeatedly to go inside the building. A few cigarettes burnt his lungs and lips, which made him look at his wristwatch.

Quarter past seven. It was that *ahorita* moment when he saw Will waving his hands from among the energetic crowd who had never slept in these streets.

*Ahorita* was a pretty vague word used in Spain. Those who really understood the thought under the skin of the people who said Ahorita in this country, did realize what it meant. It could be now, in five minutes, in fifteen minutes, or in one hour.

A friendly hug followed upon his arrival, with a very formal question.

"Que tal amigo! Did you reach so early?"

"No, I reached a few minutes back and was smoking in the corner of that building." Hari answered pointing towards the luminous entrance of Dollhouse.

"That's where we are going." Will walked towards the entrance of that heaven, hesitating to hear Hari's response. At the entrance, a guy who looked like a Paki stood right behind them. The huge bouncer in his black attire asked something to Will. The long response from Will felt just like they had known each other for years.

"What did he say?" Hari enquired

"Nah! Nothing, he asked if the person standing behind us had brought us here." Will replied.

"They are some brokers in this place, and they get paid for bringing in customers" Will explained.

"Did we have to pay extra if we told him he brought us here?" Hari's curiosity moved further.

"Nah! We don't need to"

"Then we should have told him that he brought us here; at least that man would have gained something from that."

Hari's humanity kicked in with the consciousness of how people lived in a country like his. People moved to developed countries with the hope of earning more, so that they could make their families progress, instead of just meeting the ends.. The society that lived in prosperity, in this part of the world rarely understood that. Or was that his pigeonhole thinking since he hailed from such a place? However, his consciousness dried down as soon as they walked inside through that massive door.

"Wow, it's a strip club."

"Did you like this place?" Will chuckled with a question.

"I don't know yet! But it's a good start," Hari answered, hiding his excitement.

Hari had seen so many beautiful breasts together only in porn sites he browsed to quench his manhood thirsts. This was the first time in real. There were ladies with bare tops the pole dancing like in *The Sopranos*[7]. He muddled on what to see or where to see. Varieties of torsos were open in front of his eyes–black, brown, white, pink, and even red. He recalled the caricatured breasts that popped up on Instagram from time to time, which explained the speciality of each shape.

A moment of silence took him to the thought of why some religionists did jihad and followed the man from the desert for Jannat, or ate papers in which the preachings were written and firmly believed in the guy who was born in a barn, or followed the mitzvot to reach heaven, or wore sandalwood paste on their forehead and followed a bunch of books to reach *swarg*?

The commonality was, Jannat, swarg or heaven, they all had beautiful women constantly roaming around you like bees around its hive with nectar. Dollhouse was just identical to those places. Then why did they have to kill people to reach there. Paying a few Euros would have sufficed their needs.

"Cervesa?" Will asked.

"Si"

"Dos cervesas por favor." The guy standing near our table took a note and left after chatting with Will in gibberish.

A few moments later, a couple of women with well-shaped round breasts, covering just their nipples with a couple of small pieces of clothes attached to a string, came to our table with the beers. The pieces of cloth hiding their nipples left an opportunity for individual fantasies. They sat beside us initiating a small chat with Will in Spanish, a moment when Hari incessantly cursed himself for not learning Spanish.

The Latina who sat next to Hari tried to converse with him in bits and pieces of the colonial language she had picked up through her on-the-job experience.

The place was darker than outside where the sun had already surrendered for the day. The whole area was decorated with red, yellow, and blue blinking lights that pierced the eyes of those who sat with their drinks on unmovable metal tables with chairs that had soft feathered cushions, directed to the podium. This was to engage the customers with the pole dancers, who were inside a giant bird cage on the wide podium that was visible from any corner of the bar.

The long semi-circled counter had skilled bar tenders of all genders who were flair bartending. Behind them were numerous alcohol bottles of different colours, shapes, sizes, and varieties those Hair had never seen in his life, but only in some movies and advertisements. The loud Spanish music from Latin America made the low-decibel human conversations really difficult in that closed space. However, that closed space was never capable of invoking somebody's claustrophobia.

"What's your name, Cariño?" The Latina who sat next to Hari asked, continuing her slow up-and-down motion with her palm on his thighs.

"Hari and You?"

"[h]Ari, Yo Andrea." She never stopped her action and pushed herself closer to him. Hari was experiencing a carnal passion rushing through his blood and veins as never before.

"You should pay her something," Will whispered to Hari.

"Twenty Euros?"

"Vale, that should be fine!" Will answered

Hari took out his wallet and offered her twenty euros. Andrea moved closer to him, showed the breast squeezed between the tight, petite clothes, and signalled to place it in between them. He ensured that he touched them in the best possible way when he placed them to continue his regained carnal passion. She stood sensually, took Hari's mobile phone from the table, which was already unlocked, and typed her number.

"I will give you the best price and the best experience."

She whispered in his ears after kissing his cheeks closest to the lips and walked away slowly without losing the slightest bit of her sensuality, exhibiting her extensive skill in what she had just offered.

**Andrea Sex:** Hari saved the number on his mobile phone.

"Did you like her?" Will asked

Hari just nodded with a grin.

Will had a boyfriend, not a girlfriend, so it was understandable why he didn't want to pay the girl who sat next to him. She left his side disappointed, but a question still left inside Hari's head as a spillover: whether Will had had the same carnal passion that he felt at *Doll House*?

They continued to enjoy the artists who performed inside the bird cage, sipping the drinks one after the other, until they decided to walk out of that enormous door.

It never once stuck their mind if those pole dancers who performed inside that cage felt the same as a bird or any other animal in a zoo or a cage, until a gigantic bouncer opened the door for them. Did those bouncers stand there to stop any external risks for the dancers, or were they standing to prevent the dancers from leaving the cage whenever they liked?

Whatever they experienced now, wasn't that an objectification of women or an ambient output of human trafficking of poor women from third-world countries?

They danced to make their lives meet the ends or for someone who lived in their poor countries who expected a money order cheque at the beginning of each month.

Did they dance nude by choice or were they trapped once and could never get out? Did anyone ever care about their health or well-being? Weren't they the result of a patriarchal society that was seen when you looked out of your window anywhere in this world, with just variable intensities?

Thousand more questions were there to be asked; however, Hari and Will walked out of that enormous decorated brown door as if nothing had happened in this world except for triggering one of their carnal passions.

Cigarettes were lit again, and the night slowly departed when they moved their steps in different directions toward their nests, where they ultimately slumbered with heavy doses of alcohol and carnal passions.

***

*I don't think this is going to work between us anymore.*

Suddenly, when everything felt normal, a text message from Devi without having the prefixes *good morning darling,* triggered a bell in the devil's gadget in a morning.

Hari woke up from his bed in shock, trying to comprehend what happened. Even last night, they both went to bed after a long call with nothing but intimacy, discussion about long distance, and mostly silence.

"What has changed overnight? Love is on when fighting continues; when silence creeps in, it stops. It's like the armrest in a car; you feel it when you don't have one." Hari murmured inwardly.

For him, it beheld as a regular fight provoked by something he had not discovered yet. He took a moment. Without responding to anything, as taught by his shrink during his sessions for treating anger issues, he continued his morning routine.

Philosophically, Love has a language spoken through heart and eyes. Reality was antagonistic. It was always challenging to understand what's in the other person's heart. Keeping away from that uncertainty was not something effortlessly doable.

Hari made back-to-back calls to Devi, who would already be under the heat of the sun at noon, but to no avail.

*You there, darling?*

Two blue ticks appeared immediately on his screen.

*Don't call me that. I can't forgive you for what you have done to me.*

*I still don't understand what's wrong.* Hari responded promptly.

*Where were you last Friday night?*

Last Friday night, he was with Will at the Dollhouse. Was that what she was asking? He probed himself. How come she knew about that? Only Will knew about it; there was no way in this world that Will would have spoken to her about it. Hari tried to calm himself down.

*Please pick up my call. I don't know what you are talking about, so let's not talk through text.*

Texting, especially when angry, could kill a relationship or make it worse – something he learned the hard way years back after a series of unfortunate events. Right after a double blue tick on the text, he dialled again, and this time, the video call was picked up by Devi.

She looked at her worse—her eyes were swollen due to intense weeping. Cheeks were so red that it could have blasted a stream of blood anytime, like a balloon that was filled to its maximum potential, the eyeliner spread and showed the exact path in which her tears flowed down. A penetrating silence burst into an interrogation that set Hari's teeth on edge.

"Where were you last Friday night?"

"I was with Will," Hari responded.

"I meant exactly after seven o'clock at night, I know where you went and what you did!" The anger of Devi was fuming beyond his expectations

"Yeah, I went to a club with Will."

"What club? Wasn't that a brothel? Did you have sex with someone called Andrea?" Devi was steaming.

"What? I didn't have sex with anyone; yeah, we went to a strip club, not a brothel."

"No, you are lying. I have proof."

"Proof! What proof?"

Visiting a strip club was a man's curiosity, and there was no sex involved. What was she talking about?

During a forest fire, only running towards the wind would save. Telling her what happened might remove unwanted thoughts from her mind. But how did she know all these? He wondered.

Once again, Hari tried explaining the same old wine story.

"No, you are lying. You went to a brothel and had sex with someone called Andrea."

Devi was not ready to listen to any bit of information he shared.

"How can you cheat me like this? Tell me?" She continued.

An array of repeated arguments continued, bringing more clarity into the picture. She knew where he went, when he went, how he went, how long he stayed, whose numbers were saved in his mobile, whom he called, for how long, and…

"Was she hacking into my phone?" Hari murmured. "No, not a chance. She is not tech-savvy; she is incapable of that. Is anyone else feeding her?"

For the most complicated problems, thinking of the simplest solution was best. But Hari didn't know if he had to think about a solution to—*what she argued about or for stalking him using the technology*.

Data privacy was always a myth, just like God. The simplest solution at that point was to improve his data security by changing the passwords of all those systems created by *Larry Page, Mark Zuckerberg*[8], and others in the web world. Thus, creating a more significant barrier for unnecessary transparency in their relationship.

Love and respect couldn't be bought. It just happens. You might be the perfect one, but people never look for a perfect person. They look for a suitable person.

Hari looked imperfect for a person born in a society constructed with moral codes defined by religions, without respecting the needs of humans, but the fear of the almighty. Rejection from Devi echoed his emotions with a sense of redirection.

No relationship could be identified during its best time, but only when it becomes terrible. The room for unforgivable mistakes filled Devi's heart, when Hari's revolved around his freedom, privacy, and curiosity. He needed a friend who didn't lose her friendship with him even after falling in love. He felt as if he lost that with Devi, even though he failed, feared, and succumbed to the fact that he should have communicated and set the right expectations with her.

People learn to stand up only if they fall again, again and again. They discussed, argued, fought, and convinced each other a million times. Hari was the first to quote it as a toxic relationship and decided to break up. The fear of Hari leaving her panicked Devi; it was not what she wanted.

Then what exactly did she want?

The following days were arguments to convince Hari to return to her life, for which he seemed determined not to. She argued, pleaded, and tried to persuade him a million times.

The last question of that unended epic of love was;

Whose mistake was that?

Hari being at Doll House or Devi, who stalked him by hacking into his privacy?

Who needed to convince whom, for what?

Whose appeal to pity fallacy was it in the end?

The discussions, arguments, and convincing dried up slowly when he stopped responding to the calls and texts. She never called again to ask what he thought, instead of what he felt.

All over the world, people fall in love. They pine, live, die, or even kill for love. They stop hearing each other, speaking only through their eyes and hearts. When people fall for each other, they search for reasons in each other to love more and stay connected. When they start falling apart, they search for reasons to hate each other. Often, the characters they had seen in each other as virtues would turn hostile, and sometimes vice versa, based on what the brain decoded or wanted.

- Even if your heart will be torn out of your chest for some time, move away from the toxic stuff.
- Why are you with someone who cannot trust you?
- Why are you with someone who cannot give you what you want and you cannot give what she wants?
- You don't deserve to live like this.

Throughout his era of grand separation, he repeatedly heard these statements from the close ones; however, it was better to stay quiet when everyone had an opinion.

- Toxicity
- Controlling
- No respect for personal space
- Trauma bonding

During the entire breakup infection window, more words and sentences from the thesaurus of love appeared before him. Everyone was spot on, but what did he need?

Hari never thought about it; instead, he tried to find ways to move on with his life in a *Utopia*[9] where everything was perfect, harmonious, and free from conflict, suffering, or injustice.

Emotions could never be experimented. It was better to take a step back and think about what he really needed. Rather than searching for miracles, he should have taken slow and steady steps towards contentment.

The *good morning darling* messages from Devi did not wake him up ever after. There were no video calls that extended for hours that contained virtual coitus or prolonged unspoken silent gazing at each other. He wished everything was a dream. His ego never let him call her back either.

# II

# Street Life & The Phone of Hope

"Why do you think I should try to meet her after 8 months?" Hari asked Liz with a trembling sound

"This is the exact reason why you should meet her. You either need a closure or a restart. You are still standing where she has left you. Whatever! I can't tell what should be your choice? But you need to meet her and understand where she stands after these months if you want to move ahead with your shitty life. You can't live on like this forever. Didn't you know that she had trust issues before committing to her? You did, right?

Then why did you commit? You may have seen many more virtues in her, that overshadowed her other behaviours. Right?

Book your tickets and get your ass out of here as soon as you can. Speak to her and come back with or without her. You can't keep carrying her like a shadow.

And now, I want you to sing lemon tree along with them."

Liz asserted with conviction, determination, and emotional intensity apparently she had it in the store for aeons.

"I need to think about it," Hari replied.

"Yes, please!" Liz quit the topic and gave another strong response.

"I wonder how, I wonder why, yesterday, you told me about the blue, blue sky and all that I can see…"

They hummed along and continued their walk towards the L' Ovella Negra.

The entrance to that dungeon— L' Ovella Negra was still protected by two gigantic men in their smart black attire called bouncers. One of them opened the heavy door like turning a page of a book.

It looked like a prison under an old castle, reminding one from the Roman Empire, with ancient broken brick walls. However, they looked strong enough for the enormous rock-like structure seen on the roof.

The bar lit incandescently. People sat around casks on wooden chairs as if they were sailing in the Mediterranean Sea to explore and colonize the rest of the world. Anyone who walked in would expect to see servers dressed like pirates or knights at the bar counter. But, they were wearing ultra-modern, thin clothes that stuck to their bodies.

In a dark corner were two huge foosball tables bigger than the ones in Hari's office pantry. One Euro silver was seen on the table corners, indicating someone had already blocked the table for the next game.

After a couple of steps ahead, it felt like entering a new room inside an old Roman castle—the room resembled an assembly area for the Senatus Romanus, where the aristocrats of the empire would have probably met. There was a big pool table where people gathered around, which was no less than the foosball table in the other room. After climbing five to six stairs, a few steps ahead were the bar counter and the toilets—that once again reminded a carnival ground.

"Una jarra de cerveza, por favor." Liz didn't wait to ask what Hari wanted.

"Fine?" She continued, looking at Hari. Was that really a question or confirmation?

"I will take a pulled pork hamburgesa, por favor" Hari's Spanglish was well accepted in these bars due to its international customer nature.

The girl at the counter smiled and asked them to wait on the side of that counter after swiping the card. A jar of beer, a pulled pork burger, two glasses, and a bowl of popcorn followed.

Finding a place to sit was more of a struggle than searching a needle in the hay. After roaming inside the bar for a few minutes, they found a place to sit with a Mexican lady and her flatmate who spoke non-stop in Spanish, for which Hari just nodded and Liz answered the most.

Hours passed like a click of the finger before they decided to leave the place after completing two jars of beer, a couple of rounds of losing the foosball, and the Instagram IDs of the couple who shared the space with them. The slow walk towards the metro station was mainly filled with conversation about the evening and everything in the backlog.

*Ayudame por favor*

A handwritten board and paper cup were waiting in front of the passers-by to drop some silver, which was almost empty. But what hit their eyes was the man who sat behind those. He was covered in a vast blanket to save himself from the cold, someone who looked like he was in his forties. He had an iPhone with Air Pods in his ears playing the voice of the video he was watching. He behaved like he was least bothered about the board and the cup which unveiled an arrogance. iPhone, Air Pods, pavement bed, paper cup, board; no more mismatch was needed evoke Hari's curiosity. The only thing that matched the begging was his beard and a look that gave a feeling of not having taken a bath or shaved for a few days. Anyway, there was no stinking scent around him.

They walked past him, and then Hari turned around to stare momentarily at him.

"He has an iPhone and Air Pods and doesn't know what else. Still begging?"

"Barcelona is weird and interesting simultaneously," Liz replied with a grin.

"Come, let's go," she continued.

"I need a minute." Hari started walking back those few steps they advanced earlier

"Come with me, wonder if he speaks English."

"Are you going to speak to him?" Liz asked

"Yep, seems interesting. What if he has a story for the world?"

Before completing the conversation, they were already in front of him. This time, Hari made a much closer look. His blanket was neither old nor worn. His dress did not look like a regular street panhandler. The beard was not grown out of lack of facilities; it was well groomed, and the hair was well set. On a typical day, he would have been found inside an apartment near Eixample doing something interesting, but today didn't seem normal for him.

"Señor! Hablas Ingles?"

"Yes, I do." He replied to Hari's question with a neutral accent, which guaranteed he knew how to use that language with ease.

"May I sit here?" Hari asked, to which he nodded. Liz preferred to continue standing and observing where it would take them.

"Did you eat something?" Hari asked.

"No, I haven't."

"Alright! Please give me a few minutes."

Hari neither said his plan nor waited for his answer. He caught Liz by her hand and started walking toward the *McD*[10] right across the road.

"Do you want to buy him food?" Liz asked

"He looks so genuine. I want to know him better, and the best way to start that is through his stomach."

Hari answered and continued to his destination without knowing his or the man's destiny.

They bought two burgers and a drink in a few minutes, followed by a haste walk back to his roadside home.

"Here you go!" Hari handed over the paper bag to the man and sat next to him without asking his permission this time. Liz continued to stand.

"If you don't mind, can I ask you a question?" The man only nodded to his question while unwrapping one of the burgers and the cola.

"Señor, you have an iPhone and Air Pods and look like you come from a well-off background. Maybe circumstances have brought you here; however, you could have just sold the Air Pods or iPhones to find some food. right?

You are here! On the streets, what's more important than living for another day?"

The man chuckled, "Do you want my phone?"

"No, no, I am so curious to understand why you are here."

Hari stopped and the man started speaking.

"Sometimes people we love don't love us or stop loving us back. It can cause vast pain. Life is full of surprises; sometimes, we meet someone who feels the same way, appreciates us for who we are, and might climb up Mount Everest for us irrespective of all our flaws. But what if you again lose those battles for lust. How many times will it come and go?

Relationships should be about connecting, building trust, adapting to each other, and being consistent. No two human beings are perfect for each other; it's all about understanding and adapting to each other's imperfections without making many changes in one's life.

Perhaps, I failed in the last part of it. I lost a battle.

Until a few days back, I had a wife, a beautiful daughter, a home, and a lot. Unfortunately, I didn't value them when I had them. Lust blinded my eyes, and now I am here."

When he finished talking, they could see the man's eyes brimming with tears. Hari touched his palms to console him.

"Señor! We all make mistakes; we are humans. I don't want to ask you what happened because I think it will take you back to the memories you don't want. When we saw you a few minutes back, you were at least enjoying your moment by watching something on your phone.

Just stay happy, and things will fall into place.

But you have yet to answer my first question. I don't want to force you, but I was pretty fascinated to see someone like you in the streets."

Hari was so careful with his choice of words to avoid hurting him more.

"Do you know what's in my bag?"

"No," Hari answered sarcastically, thinking how he would know what was inside his bag.

The man opened the bag and showed it to him. It was full of books, manuscripts, and other stationery.

"I am a writer. I used to write content for magazines. But after COVID-19, I lost my job and started working as a freelancer, which did not earn me enough. I could not pay my share of the mortgage, nor could I pay for my daughter. I had to live with my wife's salary."

Wife's salary?

Nature creates diversity, not hierarchy or inequality, but society transforms this diversity into discrimination and inequality. What was wrong with the wife's salary? If a wife can live on husband's salary, why can't it be the other way around.

Men could never be equal to men, too. Even though this might sound weird, the truth was always harsh. A black man or a white one. The one in a wheelchair and the one that can run—a known pity that men still have the pressure to earn in our present society irrespective of their status quo.

The height difference between husband and wife. Men's loneliness, accompanied by the social epitome of 'not to cry,' forces them into depression, suicide, and crimes—a kind of emotional castration. A man cannot cry even when his mom dies in this society. Men's loneliness should be a feminist issue.

Patriarchy or Matriarchy could destroy both men and women. It would dehumanize the entire humanity. End of the day what the world need is equity.

The man continued. "At some point, I became unfaithful to my wife. Perhaps she also started seeing someone else. Here, it becomes irrelevant who did what.

What does a relationship bring to you, the urge or the power to go to a different level or do something creative in life? But we lost our communication. The ego emerged so sturdily that we stopped trying to fix things. My arrogance made me feel so powerful that I thought I would diminish that with her. What I thought love was just lust.

She asked me to leave the house and also got a restraining order against seeing my daughter. I had no money to pay rent, so I was litigated from the place I moved to, and now I am sleeping on the streets.

I hope she forgives me one day and calls me back.

My only hope is this phone; I have faith that I will get work someday, which will help me put my life back together, and for that, people should be able to reach me. If I sell this, my existence in this world will be wiped out forever."

The man's pain travelled across the hearts of Liz and Hari through his trembling voice. Hari hugged him until he calmed down. They stood like that for a few seconds.

"I'm so Sorry! I feel very sorry for you. I hope your life gets back on track soon."

Hari stood up, and Liz hugged him so tightly, sharing the pain across his nerve cells as electrical impulses, that was strong enough to burn them down to ashes. The atmosphere filled with blue everywhere under the black sky.

"Quality of life is not materialistic; it's how we present ourselves. People want to see themselves as powerful. Sometimes, being around someone might diminish that urge to power. But the truth is, it all comes from one's self. The anxiety about the future kills the future, but that doesn't mean we don't worry about the future. A sense of accomplishment comes only from self-love, and that comes from futuristic achievements. However, for a consistent feeling of selflove, we should feel loved and express love." Hari concluded his sentiments to Liz.

The goodbye was very soft and humble among them. The next 100meter walk to Passeig de Gracia metro was total silence except for the noise of the tourists and vehicles from the surroundings.

"I will book the ticket to India tonight. I want to meet her. Let me face it."

Hari broke the silence at the metro station's entrance, at the end of their walk.

"Sure! I will see you after I am back from London. Keep me updated. Good luck to you." Liz hugged him again, expressing her sincere joy at a friend's attempt to progress in his love life.

Thus, the hope of survival triggered the hope of revival.

# III

# The Ultimate Chapter of Drama

Thank you for flying with us

The last words from the captain reminded Hari that the journey of thirteen hours, including a layover, had come to an end. He took the only backpack he was carrying from the overhead compartment. His mind was entirely blank, struggling to create the right emotions for the moment, like a writer's block—you never know what to write. Overcoming the challenge would require writing without caring about the outcome, even if it might turn out as gibberish.

He had ambitions, he was passionate about many things, he had goals set for long and short terms, and he craved for achievements and friends. But what did she have? Nothing, no hobbies or friends? Devi was no different from many girls who chose to have nothing apart from the love of their life, revolving around them like nothing else existed in this world.

But if that love was accompanied by an inability to trust, it hurt the relationship.

*Love without trust is like an unfermented wine that is merely grape juice with a lot of sugar; you enjoy the first sips, not later. Love accompanied by trust is the real wine that always get better over time.*

There were always options to fix instead of flee. During the worst situations, you should start looking at people from a distance and learn how beautiful they were. As long as they were looked upon from a very close distance, they would look like giants. Look at the partners through a rearview mirror every now and then to reiterate the beauty and character you fell for.

Hari, reached his home town Trivandrum. A small town in the beautiful state of Kerala, at the southernmost tip of the Indian peninsula that was famous for its serene beauty, lush green landscape, backwaters, health, social and education indices equivalent to European nations. It's movies and politics always contradicted with the rest of the country. The serenity of the place didn't make him feel home unlike every other time he visited this place.. There was no one to wait for him at his house, after Devi left both his heart and home. The tuk-tuk dropped him at his doorstep after long conversation about potholes, petrol prices, governments, the new Ram mandir at Ayodhya, the upcoming election, etc. Although Hari was keenly interested in all these discussions and stamped his authority with inevitable participation always, this time it was just soft humming and nodding.

As It was pretty late at night, no neighbours noticed him turning on the lights and unlocking the door, which avoided his bombardment with curious questions to understand if he had lost the job or left Spain ultimately or Why returning so early when he left only a few months back or was there any of his relatives in death bed or dead or where has Devi gone as they haven't seen her for months; followed by advices to rent the house and not leave it vacant, to keep a servant for watering the plants or the stories about the coconut those fell after drying down, etc. All he could converse with, were some new spiders who wove their webs across almost every corner of the living room. He realized that the refrigerator had been running for months with no one to open its door, and the invertor was thoroughly dried down on distilled water, exactly resembling his thoughts.

Hari sat in his living room with no sound apart from the crickets, which were always there irrespective of the seasons, and the long howl of the street dogs who intended to disturb the sleep of the people living nearby as revenge for their ill-treatment during the day. The room was still filled with furniture, which had not been used in the past months since Devi had left the house after breaking up with him. The grey textured wall with a huge television in the middle still looked fresh, presumably some souls were watching their favourite TV shows at night. Dust was visible on the wooden teak chairs. The clock stopped running someday at half past nine, unsure whether it was in the morning or at night. The oversized couch he sat on emitted enough dust to sneeze several times. He didn't feel like getting up from there and walking upstairs to his bedroom, where there were photos of Devi and him together. He didn't dare to break his heart again tonight. He looked at his mobile phone, the time read a quarter to three. He pulled out a bed sheet from his bag spread over the couch and went to sleep along with a bunch of questions without answers, a lot of dust, lizards, spiders, crickets, and many other insects who occupied and owned the house during the human absence.

"Hari"

He woke up from his deep sleep of jet lag, hearing the yell of an old female voice. He looked at the mobile. It was switched off. He slowly got up from the couch and opened the door.

Rema Aunty, his neighbour in her sixties, was standing outside the gate.

"Son, I knew someone came here after seeing the door lamp on. Thought it should be you. When did you come?"

"I came last night, aunty," Hari answered

"Was there any urgency?"

"No, Aunty. I have some government work to finish regarding the tax, so I must be physically present. Just for two days, and I fly back to Spain," Hari tried to stop the series of questions that was about to start with a harmless lie.

"Where is that kid, Devi? Haven't seen her here for a few months."

"Uff! Can't stop this questioning ever." Hari soliloquized.

"She has gone to her mom's place. Her mom is not in the best of health now." Another lie, and Hari tried to close the conversation.

"Poor girl! Anyways, let me know if you need anything, son," She replied.

"What is the time?" Hari asked.

"It should be around eleven, eleven-thirty," Rema Aunty answered and smiled.

"Oh shit! I am getting late. Will talk once I am back." Hari rushed inside as if he had a myriad of errands to run.

Rema Aunty slowly walked towards her house, which was right opposite to his.

Hari plugged his mobile to charge and moved upstairs to the bathroom for a shower. He could not find any photos of them on the wall. Devi might have taken them down before leaving. Throughout the shower, he kept thinking about his modus operandi for meeting her.

*Devi, I am in town. I want to meet you. In fact, I came for two days to just meet you* – The WhatsApp message turned into two blue ticks in less than thirty seconds. He couldn't see her display picture; she might have deleted his number or restricted him from seeing that.

*Why now? I was toxic for you, I begged, I told you that I can't live without you. You were not there to hear. Why now?* Her reply was instant.

*Let's meet and talk; I will wait for you near the famous Chai-chai in Lulu Mall. I will be there from half past twelve, waiting for you.*

There was no response from Devi, which did not discourage Hari from getting ready and reaching the mall five minutes before he committed.

*Hope is stronger than fear*

Time took its slowest pace; the blue board of Chai-chai pierced into his eyes as he stared at them non-stop. The crowd in the mall said out loudly how cheerful the Saturday evening was; there were long queues in front of the restaurants in the food court and the movies. Children ran around carelessly dropping their ice creams and chocolate along with the adults who did the same. A bunch of housekeeping staffs in their red uniform did not seem to fail once in cleaning them off the floor instantly, apart from taking away the soiled plates, coffee mugs, tea cups, leftovers and the forgotten stuff from the food court tables, followed by a clean wipe of them. Everything looked robotic.

In some families, the headman wore the traditional attire of long white cloth, called "mundu" wrapped around the waist and simple plain or checked shirts and walked in the front. The lady of the family followed him with the children. Groups of teenagers howled and screamed, like it was the best way to have fun. Most unmarried couples intertwined their palms, challenging the conservative outlook of that society; when some didn't as they were scared of what if their families come to know about the relationship. Mostly due to the differences in caste, religion, or social and financial status.

A huge crowd was seen in front of the supermarket as if it was black Friday or the things were given away for free. Another huge crowd was seen in front of the television screen enjoying and celebrating the T20 cricket match between India and Australia; their noise, screaming, and exclamations were intermittent based on the outcome of every shot an Indian batter played.

Time continued to pass like a tortoise for Hari. He looked at the watch, and it was already one o'clock. Culturally, ahorita existed here as well, similar to Spain; however, on this occasion, he was unsure if Devi would even make it.

"Hi"

Hari turned around to see Devi standing right beside him, beautifully dressed in her black tees and blue jeans. Her slightly curly hair was straightened. Her nails were colourfully painted in purple, with enviably decorated eyes with dark blue eyeliner. She wore a pair of white shoes with golden linings and a pair of earrings that reminded the ring from Lord of the rings with magical powers to melt a man from the foot. Her *bindi* – the black dot on the centre of her forehead, doubled the complexion of her face.

"Hi"

Hari stood up from his seat and helped the lady into the chair opposite him like a gentleman; there were no kisses, hugs, or even handshakes.

A moment of silence blacked out everything around them—No traditional men or their families, couples, teenagers, kids, housekeepers, staff, or anything. The whole space seemed filled with empty chairs, dark corners, low light, and pin-drop silence.

"Why did you want to meet me after such a long time? What changed your mind? Why did you come back now? Do you want to break my heart again? I know how hard it was for me to move on; now that I have found peace of mind, you are back again. I don't know if I can help you now."

Devi threw a bunch of arguments and questions at his face, vending out her frustration in a voice that anyone from the nearby table would have curiously noticed.

"Sorry"

When he said this, his eyes started filling with the truthful nectar of emotions that kept whispering to his beating piece of flesh behind the rib cage, that reacted on every moment of his life.

"I don't know what else to say! I hurt you; in fact, we both hurt each other. I should have tried to fix it instead of running away from you. It's my mistake. You tried to come back many times, but my arrogance always kept me on the back foot. I couldn't move an inch from where I had left."

He stopped for a moment.

"Hari, I think it's too late. I don't think I can love you as I used to. I am a different person now; I want to do things in my life. I want to buy a house and travel around the world. I can't do this anymore."

"Wasn't that very easy for you?" Hari replied with a sarcastic grin.

"No, it wasn't, but I don't know if I have the same emotions left in me for you."

"I came all the way from Barcelona for two days, only to meet you. To see if we can still be there for each other. Can we spend some time together today and tomorrow until I leave, to decide if there is still a chance?" Hari proposed.

"Why do you think I should do that? Things that have to end have to end."

"Some hopes are like that. We will keep expecting, but it never happens because we never try, and we cannot love anyone without having a risk called heartbreak. If there are no other reasons, I am just pleading with you—two days, and in case we fail, I will go back without a reason to come back to this city anymore," Hari interrupted.

"I pleaded with you, not once, twice, or thrice." Devi broke out into tears.

Hari swiftly stood up from his chair opposite Devils and moved to the one beside her. He hugged her, her face pressed against his chest, causing her dark blue eyeliner to smudge across his white shirt. She hugged him back with the same intensity.

The entire mall brightened up, with the moral society staring at their shameless act in public, with contempt. It was nothing but a hug of an unsexual emotional eruption. But nothing bothered Hari or Devi.

Getting back together looked so easy for a moment.

"Come on! Let's take a walk."

Hari intertwined her palms while she rested her head on his shoulders, gratified to have mended something broken for eight months in less than eight minutes—the magic of physical presence.

"I am hungry"

"Me too"

It didn't matter who said that first; their next stop was their favourite vegetarian restaurant, which had a separate space in the food court of that shopping mall.

As usual, Devi led the ordering process. She ordered a couple of dosas—the Indian pancakes, usually slimmer than the western pancakes, banana fritters—locally called pazhampori, and south Indian filter coffee.

"My house was full of dust and spider webs. I slept on the couch in the living room. I reached really late last night and couldn't clean even a bit. I have to go back and clean the house a bit, at least to satisfy my borderline OCD so I can sleep peacefully tonight." Hari said.

"Hmm," Devi responded "Did you take all the photos with you?"

"No, they are in the cupboard inside your bedroom," Devi once again responded sublimely, indicating that our bedroom changed to your bedroom in eight months, a confident statement of where we stood.

"Would you come with me to my house today? Let's leave tomorrow together when I go to the airport."

"Do you think that's a good idea? And I can't believe you came all the way down only to see me!"

Hari responded to both the question and the statement by kissing on her palm.

"What if I was not here in town? It would have been a waste, right? You could have texted or called me."

"What if you did not respond to my texts or calls?" Hari asked and continued. "I wanted to take my chance; I thought things might improve if I met you."

Many what-ifs followed during that conversation, but they never spoke about anything that happened in the past. There was nothing left to discuss as it was discussed, argued, and fought over a million times since the doll house incident.

After roaming around for some more time, Hari drove Devi's small white car to his house without seeking any permission from her, whether she wanted to stay with him that night and the next day or forever. Things looked like they were taken for granted. Throughout driving, Hari imitated his driver of the tuk-tuk from last night, who kept talking about the potholes in the road, corrupt politicians, upcoming elections, etc. In no time, they reached the white gate of his house, which seldom looked white these days due to the dust accumulated on that. Devi stepped out and opened the gate with a clear expression of how dusty it was. She opened her palms and showed it to him how dirty it had become by just touching it, for which he chuckled.

"Devi, long time no see," The peeping lady from the opposite house, Rema Aunty, curiously asked.

"Hello, aunty, I was at my mom's place; she is not in her best shape these days."

Devi answered with a smile and expressed her busy schedule by suddenly moving on with other activities such as clearing the way for the car to park, removing the hose that was used to water the plants on the parking floor, moving the spilt-over footwear from the way of the vehicle, and so on.

Hari wondered why they both gave her the same answer. Was that the mental synchronization they always had or a mere coincidence? But why did Rema's aunty ask the same question to Devi—crooked or satisfying her moral obligation to learn about the neighbours' secrets, pains, and pleasures, or just casual and coincidence, or was she searching for another blockbuster gossip for their kitty parties? They walked inside, ignoring the presence of that old lady quite swiftly, as if something was burning inside the oven.

Hari didn't seem to startle Devi as he approached from behind and wrapped his arms around her in a hug. He kissed the back of her neck, cheeks, and ears before slowly turning her around.

Their lips met, tongues intertwined, breaking all the barriers and flooding each other's mouths, rediscovering every missed taste over the last eight months. The kiss was so deep that it seemed to mock the nonfunctional clock on the wall, which was powerless to measure its duration. His palms searched her body for something he missed. When it was about to trigger a rhapsody of coitus, she stopped him.

"I think we should clean the house a little so we can sleep peacefully at night."

Devi woke him from a dream which he awaited to see for eight months.

*Why?*

*Maybe she is still not ready, or perhaps she needs more time.*

Hari ran a series of questions inside his head, but respected her choice.

A few sneezing moments later, the bed was decorated with fresh bedsheets, pillow covers, and blankets from the cupboard—emanating a musty odour. Sweeping the room, followed by a jasmine room spray, brought a refreshing fragrance, enveloping the entire space in freshness.

"It's already half past ten. The cleaning took too much time. My head is breaking with jet lag. Maybe we should sleep."

Hari mentioned with a smile that was missing from his lips before he met her.

The lights were turned off, and they huddled together inside the blanket. Although the bed lamps were non-functional, the faint light that seeped in through the window like a voyeur, illuminating the room sufficiently for them to gaze into each other's eyes. No words were exchanged as their lips and tongues intertwined again. The garments that separated their bare bodies were removed from their path. They caressed each other in such a way that they forgot the long gap without any exchanges. His fingers took turns reaching out to every inch of her body before they reached her lips between the thighs, which were moist than a jelly.

"Stop, Hari, I can't do this." She interrupted once more.

Hari conducted no interrogations. Instead, he laid on his back calmly, watching the ceiling fan spin rapidly, casting a translucent shadow on the rough surface above. For a few minutes, he heard nothing apart from the hissing of a mosquito near his ear. Devi laid hugging him, with her head on his chest, trying to listen to every beat of his heart, while he ran his fingers through the strands of her hair. In no time, the souls confused about this new start also dived into total silence, along with their tired bodies.

The morning sunlight pierced through the windows, rousing him from his jet-lagged slumber into a fresh physical and romantic awakening. The kitchen was just decorative as it had not been used since she left the house. Hence, he ordered coffee and breakfast through the modern-era food delivery app that served people 24x7. They laid in the bed, hugging each other under the scorching sun, mixing their sweat until the delivery boy rang the doorbell. Hari put on his pyjamas and ran downstairs to collect the delivery, along with a small tip for the boy who kicked off another happy day of his life.

When Devi came into his life, **I became WE**. Then, the **WE** started dreaming about a world that could be built together—visualizing it through each other's eyes. People left with genuine feelings for someone from the past, should wait to shut themselves down until they find out, what can be done with their leftover feelings.

For Devi and Hari, it was more of a rebuilding with those leftovers.

"Hon! Wake up. It's already eleven O'clock. We just have this day, and Yo voy."

Devi didn't understand the Spanish phrase, she wasn't too concerned about it either; instead, she woke up with a stretch and extended that to pull Hari towards her, to kiss his lips gently. Followed by a short washroom routine, they once again gathered at the dining table to finish off the hot Idlies (the famous steam cake made from rice and black lentils, a traditional breakfast), and chutney delivered by the app people. They sipped their coffees, which were reheated in the microwave, which was the only cooking appliance that remained free of mould or fungus.

"My flight is at midnight; I must leave around nine O'clock." Devi just hummed for a response.

Cleaning was never a part of their day's agenda. It just happened as they both hated dust and webs.

Dusting the entire house, washing the floor, watering the plants, pulling out the weeds, and kissing every five minutes; overall, the tasks of two hours extended to three due to the intermittent display of affection. Neither of them was keen about the events in each other's lives, during the dark period of their separation. Time travelled back in its original form, of how it was before the Doll house incident.

Food and juices were ordered again through the delivery service that arrived on time; however, the feasting fell beyond the Spanish or the Indian lunch hours, still followed by a siesta—a resting ritual after lunch in Spain. For a few hours, the laughter, fun, sensuality, emotional drama, and hard work came to a halt.

"I have to go. I need to meet someone, and I want to tell you something before I leave."

Hari, who slept deeper due to tiredness, embracing his returned love of life, was awakened by Devi with a whisper in his ears.

"Now? I have to catch the flight in a few hours. Shall we leave together?"

Devi got up from the bed and walked towards the dining room without answering his question. In a few moments, when Hari reached downstairs, she was waiting with a cup of coffee that she ordered through the delivery service while he was asleep. The app people were the only ones who visited them that day, that too thrice.

*I want to tell you something before I leave* from Devi resonated like the temple chimes from his childhood memories. His fear of the news she was about to break smelled like the turmeric, coconut oil, and milk from the offerings made to the snakes.

"I am seeing someone; I don't know what to tell you. I shouldn't have come here with you last night. I shouldn't have kissed or let you..." She stopped without completing the sentence.

But she did. Hari remained stunned; it was totally unexpected. Deep in his mind, he thought of it much before booking the flight from Barcelona itself. The entire fear was replaced by happiness the last two days, not by imagination, but by the reality that was right in front of him.

"She could have said that earlier, or maybe she is not sure about the relationship, or maybe she loves me more than him," Hari said to himself.

"I should have told you, but I couldn't. When I met you yesterday at the mall, I lost control and felt like I was regaining the old me. I still love you. But I am still determining what I am going to tell him. He is waiting for me on the beach. I have not gotten into something serious with him yet. But he is, of course, serious with me. Yesterday, before I met you, I told him I would meet you. I didn't tell him that I would stay with you. But in the last two days, I realized that I still love you and I can't love anyone more than you. At first, it was hatred for leaving me. I pleaded with you to come back, but you never did."

After a short pause, Devi continued.

"I need to speak to him. Anyways, you fly back safely. Let's talk once you reach."

Hari gazed up at her with an emotionless face, from which the blood had entirely been drained out. His hands and feet became colder than a dead man's. His pupils dilated, letting out all the light around him in that luminous room. His lips turned drier and drier each second. There was no strength left to pick up the coffee mug, which was half empty. He held on to the ear of that mug as if it was protecting him from falling. His heartbeat was never heard or felt anymore. He wondered if he was turning into a zombie, and he was just moments away from his complete transformation.

"Why don't you say something?" Devi's eyes conveyed her dilemma when she shouted that.

"Okay!" He replied.

A complete silence filled the atmosphere. Devi took her car keys and walked outside, looking at him, expecting to follow, and he did. The car didn't start making the situation more dramatic, like even the car didn't want her to go. She tried once, twice, thrice, and more without any avail.

"I think there is some starting trouble," she said.

Hari could not move to open the bonnet or check the problem; instead, he just hummed softly.

"Do you want to walk with me to the road? I can take a taxi from there. I will come back tomorrow morning with a mechanic and get this fixed. You leave the gate unlocked. After I take the car, I will leave the key with Rema, Aunty." She proposed like no heart-tearing discussions happened between them.

He hummed again and walked her to the road—the longest, quietest walk they had in the past two days. She waved at a tuk-tuk that came empty, who stopped next to them.

"Don't worry! I can't promise you anything right now. I need some time. I can't hurt people, you know that," she said.

"Do I know that?" He monologued inside.

"You fly back safely; I will call you. I still have my love for you, but..."

She did not complete it; instead, she hugged Hari so hard that it was their last hug, and kissed him deeply without any guilt statements.

The tuk-tuk vanished from his sight in a matter of seconds as if the driver was in a hurry. The return walk felt like a blind journey. Everything and everyone around him faded into darkness, like a new moon night. The aura that was around him had vanished forever. He could not feel his steps, the heat or the cold, the smell of the garbage bins, the pollens of the trees, or the machine that incessantly released huge clouds filled with nicotine against his breath, that engulfed him, brewing a thunderstorm. Since he had walked down that alley for years, his muscle memory guided him precisely to his doorstep. He was not steered by his brain. His soul continued to travel with her in the back seat of that tuk-tuk, making love and putting efforts to convince her constantly.

When he got back, the lights were left on. He picked up a few strands of her hair from the floor, not because of his borderline OCD but because they were the last remaining physical piece of her memory in that 50-square-meter house. He sniffed the jacket she wore the previous night when she felt cold, countless times, repeatedly, like a dog searching for its beloved master who was lost in the time-lapse of this world.

He was more exhausted than ever; his legs barely supported his weight. The scent of her love lips between her thighs, lingering on his left middle finger from last night. It no longer aroused his sexual desires or fantasies but nostalgia and hope. All that remained was a profound desire to time travel and keep running his time with her in an endless time loop.

She was a piece of him that he couldn't get rid of, despite the tides of emotions. He was afraid of making the wrong decision, but in the end, he found solace in taking the decision to come back for himself.

Another thirteen hours of a flight journey with a layover marked the end of a beginning.

While every love or life seemed unique, a default skeletal template existed where they intersected here and there. True happiness, however, laid not in the skeleton but in the fillings around it. To attain their potency, these fillings had to be cleared, refilled, updated, changed, topped up, or refreshed over time. Much like success, happiness could not induce dopamine if the same event was repeated again and again. Anyone could achieve this potency if there were self-love, acceptance of rejections, letting go of things & people, chasing their dreams, loving others selflessly, and never expecting anything, including gratitude in return; whatever received was a bonus.

Irrespective of the spring blossoms, the mould infestation from the roof still stared at him wildly when Hari opened his apartment door. The hope of survival, the hope of revival, and the hope of falling in love once again did not let him rest. Ignoring the most required sleep, he rushed back to feel the scent of Barcelona at her heart, Catalunya.

Nothing had changed in this city, in two days. The darkness had already hit the sky. Hence, the pigeons, the kids, or the bubblers were not seen in the square.

His life had always been an illusion in which he either overindulged or underindulged in emotions. This forced him to follow a social structure in between, which only led to sorrow, disappointments, anger, frustration, anxiety, depression, and heartbreaks. All he had to do was, connect the line between his birth and death with happiness.

*Hi Devi, I have reached.*

Succumbed to anxiety, Hari triggered his first text message to Devi from the devil's gadget.

"It is already half past ten here; she might have slept," Hari said quietly to himself, but he continued checking his mobile phone for her reply every few seconds.

He walked around the streets of Catalunya like an insane monk who had never learned to live an everyday life with an actual direction.

For her, it was just a tide when it was an ocean for him, and it hissed in his ears, waiting for the unreachable horizon from the shore.

"It's me, who made her feel special. My explanations, beautifications, colours, interpretations, and everything glorified her. It's she who has to come back to reality. There is nothing that I need to be jealous of. I don't want her to be a stranger to me."

His murmur with stranger emotions continued.

Hari's eyes searched for the man with the iPhone, who sat right across the McD. He was nowhere to be found.

Had he found work?

Had his wife taken him back?

Had he again fallen in love with someone?

Or

Had he sold his iPhone to find shelter and food?

Hari's anxiety triggered a series of questions, like birds ceaselessly circling his head. He sat precisely where the man with the phone of hope had sat, with the hope of love.

Constant gaze on the devil's gadget waiting for Devi's reply and the jet lag, slowly grew his eyelids heavier, heavier, and heavier, beyond his actual strength to hold them up any longer.

Ignoring the bone-chilling cold at the beginning of that spring, Hari slowly surrendered to his everlasting trance on that pavement.

# The Epic of Hope

# GLOSSARY

## PEANUTS

1. *Devil's gadget:* Mobile phone.
2. *Holodomor*: A man-made famine from 1932 to 1933 that killed millions of Ukrainians. Collectivization policy adopted by the Soviet government pursued most intensively between 1929 and 1933, to transform traditional agriculture and to reduce the economic power of the kulaks.
3. *Kulaks*: Prosperous peasants.
4. *Baba*: Grandmother in Ukrainian.
   *Tato*: Father.
   *Sestra*: Sister.
   *Brat*: Brother.
5. *Gulags*: Russian Corrective Labor Camps accompanying detention, transit camps and prisons that existed between the 1920s and mid-1950s.
6. *Requisition brigades:* Armed brigades sent to the villages to requisition grain by force.

## SHE IS A POEM

1. *Antoni Gaudi:* A Catalan architect from Spain, whose most notable work is Sagrada Familia.
2. *Pulp Fiction*: A Quentin Tarantino movie released in 1995.
3. *Love Actually*: A Richard Curtis movie released in 2003.
4. *What have I done? Why have I done it?*: 3 Am Wednesday by the folk-rock duo - Simon & Garfunkel.
5. *Budmo*: "let us be" a Ukrainian toast.
6. *Larry Scott and Sergey Brin*: Founders of Google.
7. *Mushrooms from the Kodai*: Hallucinating mushrooms that attract young crowds from Kodaikanal, a tourist destination from the south of India.
8. *Krasyva*: Means beauty in Ukrainian.
9. *Great dick of Barcelona*: A slang name for the building, Torre Glories.
10. *Slava Ukraini, Heroyam Slava*: Ukrainian slogans meaning Glory to Ukraine & Glory to the heroes.

## A 'KEY' STORY

1. *Take a little walk to the edge of town*: The title theme song from Peaky Blinders, a famous Netflix Television series.
2. *Da*: A slang word used by some of the languages from the south of India to call a friend or someone known who is around the same age.
3. *Deerstalker hat*: A type of hat that Sherlock Homes wore.
4. *Mr. Doyle*: Arthur Conan Doyle, the author of Sherlock Homes.
5. *Kundali, Chovva Dosham, maanglik*: A match-making Indian horoscope terminologies.
6. *Perruqueria*: Hair cutting salon in Catalan
7. *Poquito*: Means very little in Spanish slang.
8. *Kurukshetra war of Mahabharata:* A vast war fought between the cousins, Pandavas and Kauravas in the greatest Indian epic, Mahabharat.
9. *Pitamahan:* A lead character of Mahabharat.

## THE EPIC OF HOPE

1. *Sarpams*: Snake sculptures worshipped by Hindus of South India.
2. *Gillette*: Shaving blade brand that became infamous in India as a tool to commit suicide by cutting veins.
3. *Emperor of Transylvania*: Dracula.
4. *Walk of Shame*: A Russian fashion brand.
5. *I wonder how I wonder why*: Lemon Tree, a song by Fool's Garden, released in 1995.
6. *Jannat/Swarg*: Heaven.
7. *Paki*: Spanish slang for Pakistanis, mistakenly used for Indians and Bangladeshis as well.
8. *The Sopranos*: An American television series created by David Chase between 1997 to 2007.
9. *Systems created by Larry Page, Mark Zuckerberg*: Founders of Google & Facebook.
10. *Utopia*: An imaginary society that possesses highly desirable or near-perfect qualities for its member.
11. *McD*: McDonald's, the fast-food chain.

# ACKNOWLEDGEMENTS

Information on Holodomor, was gathered from Wikipedia pages and other credible online sources through randoms checks on Google.

Insights and references on Mahabharat were derived from my exposure to the epic as a child, being raised in a Hindu family.

References on relationship types were adopted from the book *Attached,* by Dr. Amir Levine & Rachel S.F. Heller, MA, published in 2010.

References of movies, television series and songs were acquired through my personal viewership of them over multiple online platforms such as Netflix, HBO and Amazon music.

For general references, my sincere thanks to all bloggers, vloggers, and influencers whose work has contributed to my research.

Scan the QR code to leave your feedback

www.ingramcontent.com/pod-product-compliance
Lightning Source LLC
LaVergne TN
LVHW030046160826
845672LV00017B/2746

* 9 7 8 8 4 0 9 6 2 5 9 5 6 *